FOREST OF SHADOWS

ALEXIS FORREST MYSTERY
BOOK 2

KATE GABLE

COPYRIGHT

Copyright © 2024 by Byrd Books, LLC. All rights reserved.

Proofreader:

Renee Waring, Guardian Proofreading Services, https://www.facebook.com/GuardianProofreadingServices

Cover Design: Kate Gable

No part of this book may be reproduced in any form or by any electronic or mechanical means, including information storage and retrieval systems, without written permission from the author, except for the use of brief quotations in a book review.

This book is a word of fiction. Names, characters, places, and incidents are either products of the author's imagination or are used fictitiously. Any resemblance to actual persons, living or dead, events, or locales is entirely coincidental. The author acknowledges the trademarked status and trademark owners of various products referenced in this work of fiction, which have been used without permission. The publication/use of these trademarks is not authorized, associated with, or sponsored by the trademark owners.

Visit my website at www.kategable.com

BE THE FIRST TO KNOW ABOUT MY UPCOMING SALES, NEW RELEASES AND EXCLUSIVE GIVEAWAYS!

Want a Free book? Sign up for my Newsletter!

Sign up for my newsletter:
https://www.subscribepage.com/kategableviplist

Join my Facebook Group:
https://www.facebook.com/groups/
833851020557518

Bonus Points: Follow me on BookBub and Goodreads!

https://www.goodreads.com/author/show/21534224.Kate_Gable

ABOUT KATE GABLE

Kate Gable is a 3 time Silke Falchion award winner including Book of the Year. She loves a good mystery that is full of suspense. She grew up devouring psychological thrillers and crime novels as well as movies, tv shows and true crime.

Her favorite stories are the ones that are centered on families with lots of secrets and lies as well as many twists and turns. Her novels have elements of psychological suspense, thriller, mystery and romance.

Kate Gable lives near Palm Springs, CA with her husband, son, a dog and a cat. She has spent more than twenty years in Southern California and finds inspiration from its cities, canyons, deserts, and small mountain towns.

She graduated from University of Southern California with a Bachelor's degree in Mathematics. After pursuing graduate studies in mathematics, she switched gears and got her MA in Creative Writing and English from Western New Mexico University and her PhD in Education from Old Dominion University.

Writing has always been her passion and obsession. Kate is also a USA Today Bestselling author of romantic suspense under another pen name.

Write her here:

Kate@kategable.com

Check out her books here:

www.kategable.com

Sign up for my newsletter:
https://www.subscribepage.com/kategableviplist

Join my Facebook Group:
https://www.facebook.com/groups/833851020557518

Bonus Points: Follow me on BookBub and Goodreads!

https://www.bookbub.com/authors/kate-gable

https://www.goodreads.com/author/show/21534224.Kate_Gable

- amazon.com/Kate-Gable/e/B095XFCLL7
- facebook.com/KateGableAuthor
- bookbub.com/authors/kate-gable
- instagram.com/kategablebooks
- tiktok.com/@kategablebooks

ALSO BY KATE GABLE

Detective Kaitlyn Carr Psychological Mystery series
Girl Missing (Book 1)
Girl Lost (Book 2)
Girl Found (Book 3)
Girl Taken (Book 4)
Girl Forgotten (Book 5)
Gone Too Soon (Book 6)
Gone Forever (Book 7)
Whispers in the Sand (Book 8)

Girl Hidden (FREE Novella)

Detective Charlotte Pierce Psychological Mystery series
Last Breath
Nameless Girl

**Missing Lives
Girl in the Lake**

ABOUT FOREST OF SHADOWS

When she finds out that the man convicted of killing her sister may be innocent, FBI agent and forensic psychologist Alexis Forrest goes on the search for the real culprit. Evidence of her sister's murder was found in a remote cabin, along with traces of dozens more young women. A serial killer has been stalking these woods for decades and he's still out there.

Alexis had returned to Broken Hill, the snowy New England town where she grew up, to investigate another case. But after finding the serial killer's cabin with evidence of other victims, she will do anything to track him down.

Meanwhile, a family is torn apart when their son goes missing while they're on a family vacation nearby. He disappears while sledding right outside of his Airbnb. The sled is found but the boy is gone. With a huge blizzard blowing in, Alexis must fight against nature and man to find the boy before all of the evidence of who took him and what happened to him is buried.

Will Alexis be able to find the boy in time? Can she find out who killed her sister before the serial killer claims another victim?

1

"**I**'m very sorry, Mr. and Mrs. Forrest, but we've identified the body as belonging your daughter, Madeline."

My eyes snap open. My body is still frozen, still half in the dream that had me in its grips a moment ago. That night. I wasn't supposed to be awake, but how was I supposed to sleep? It had been two days of constant questions and tears, phone calls, and knocks at the front door. People coming in and out, checking on my parents, bringing food, offering prayers. I couldn't sleep while Maddie was out there somewhere.

Slowly, reality seeps in and pushes the dream away. Not very far away—dreams that come from memories are like that. No doubt it will come back to haunt me.

I'm warm, I'm comfortable. It's still dark, but when I listen hard I don't hear Mitch's breathing behind me. He must have already gotten up, since his work involves heading down to the bookstore so he can bake fresh goods for the café. And I thought I was an early riser.

For a moment, it's enough to stretch beneath a heavy down comforter before rolling over to touch my nose to the pillow he slept on. It smells like his cologne—spicy, musky. I inhale deeply and smile to myself. In the middle of so much doubt and confusion, he is my constant. He's my consolation. Just like he always was when we were kids.

"Good morning."

I lift my head quickly, a little embarrassed. A tiny smile tugs at the corners of his mouth, but he says nothing about finding me with my nose buried in his pillow. "I thought you might be hungry."

"Starved," I admit, sitting up and wedging pillows behind my back before he places a tray across my legs. On it, there are scrambled eggs with chives and cheese, hash browns, and roasted tomatoes and mushrooms.

"I remember you like a savory breakfast."

"Did you make it your business to remember everything about me?"

"And if I did?" He leaves the room and returns a moment later, carrying a steaming cup in one hand, and in the other, a loaf of bread wrapped in a linen napkin.

"Fresh bread, too?" I check the clock, which reads quarter-past five. "How early did you get up?"

"It's a habit. And I left the dough to proof last night, so it was all ready to go in the oven."

It smells like heaven, and after ripping a piece off and taking a bite, I can confirm it tastes like heaven, too. "The time you spent at that baking class paid off," I manage to tell him around a mouthful of the soft, flavorful bread.

"Anything worth doing is worth doing right." I'm glad he gets up to open the curtains when he does, since I can't hide a little smile at his choice of words. He most definitely gives his all to everything he does. I can attest to that. And if I'm a little drowsy today, that would be why. For a man who gets up so early in the morning, he certainly doesn't mind staying up late …

"It's coming."

I look toward the window, where the dark sky is the only thing I can see from my vantage point. "What's it doing out there?"

"Nothing much beyond flurries. A thin coating on the ground. But if the weatherman is right, it's going to look a lot different out there this time tomorrow."

Of all times for a blizzard to announce itself. "Right while I'm neck-deep in a case. How convenient."

He throws a wry grin my way. "To be fair, when are you not on a case?"

Good point. But this one is different, and he knows that. I take another bite of the soft, warm bread, and immediately feel bad. Here we are, together after an incredible night. He went to all the trouble to make breakfast, and even popped a loaf of bread in the oven, and all I can do is complain.

But this is strange for me. Different. My last relationship ended before I officially started with the Bureau. I'm not used to this whole juggling act, trying to balance my work life and my personal life. And as Mitch has never hesitated from reminding me, I'm not very good at balance. I tend to be an all-or-nothing kind of girl, and I always have been.

"It's supposed to hit overnight, right?" I ask before taking a long gulp of the coffee.

"That's when the worst of it will fall, but as of right now they're saying it'll start blowing in during the early evening. At the worst it'll snow two inches an hour, maybe three. High winds."

"We're really going to get buried, aren't we?"

"By all reports." He sits next to me, and I notice he's not eating. He seems glad to watch me enjoy what he prepared. "I don't plan on opening the store tomorrow, and I guess we'll go from there."

"A snow day." I close my eyes and sigh. "It sounds like heaven."

He reaches out to tuck a strand of brown hair behind my ear. There's no ignoring the thrill of even a simple touch when delivered by the man in question. "Who says you can't take a snow day? They're measuring this storm in feet, not inches. There won't be much chance of getting around tomorrow, and who knows what will happen after that?"

"If I didn't know any better …" I nudge him with my blanket covered leg and grin. "I would think you were trying to convince me to take a day off with you."

"Would that be such a crime?"

"I am the expert on crime, after all …"

He leans over and presses a soft, playful kiss against my waiting lips. It tastes like coffee and sweetness. "That, you are."

Of course, my playful mood doesn't last very long. It never does lately. This is incredible, better than anything I could've imagined when I first reconnected with my high school boyfriend. I'm aware of how lucky I am that we found our way to this place, even if we haven't exactly defined where we are or what we're doing.

But I can't forget what I found yesterday, before I practically fled to Mitch's waiting arms. I needed somebody who would understand. And he did, because he always does. What happened after that … happened after that.

It doesn't change anything. There's a killer out there, too. One who might have murdered my sister. And there's another man sitting in prison for that crime.

"I'm going to have to get out to the cabin today," I announce while spearing potatoes on my fork. "Gosh, these are incredible. How did you get so much flavor into them?"

"A magician never reveals his secrets." His smile fades into a look of concern. "I guess there won't be any getting out there during the storm."

"Exactly what I was thinking."

"Do me a favor and don't stay out there too long. I'll breathe a lot easier if you're out of the woods before the first flakes fall."

"I'm not looking to take any chances." When he lowers his brow and smirks, I throw my hands in the air. "What? What's that look for?"

"You don't take chances? Did you forget I met you prior to last night? I know you a little too well."

He leans in, giving me another whiff of the coffee on his breath. I like it. "You listen to me, Agent Forrest. I want you to meet me at eight o'clock at The Tipsy Traveler, so we can have a couple of burgers before we hole up here and use the snow as an excuse to stay in bed all day tomorrow."

I can't pretend the idea is unpleasant. Or that it doesn't make me tingle more than slightly. "You'll have to play your cards right," I tease, smiling before accepting a slower, deeper kiss than the one before. The sort of kiss that promises much more than it delivers. Like a preview of what's to come.

2

Mitch's delicious breakfast bolsters me enough to head out with a clear head and an energized attitude. That, and the ticking clock. Unlike the ticking I heard in my head when Camille Martin was missing, this ticking has more to do with the first flakes of snow scheduled to fall. I want to get as much done as I can before that happens.

That means heading out to the cabin we discovered yesterday. Now that the sun has risen, the sky has gone from black to a deep, foreboding gray. Mitch was right. It's on its way, this storm. I can taste the snow in the air as I slide behind the wheel of my Corolla and wait for the heat to kick in. *Note to self: research automatic starters, ASAP.*

It's pretty clear as I look up and down Mitch's street that everybody's taking the storm seriously. A man living two doors down pops his car trunk and unloads a massive bag of rock salt, while a woman across the street opens her garage door to bring her trash cans inside rather than let them be buried.

As I head through town, I have to keep an eye out for the trucks treating the streets with brine, preparing them for the onslaught. Turning on the car's radio, it seems all I can find are reports of the storm. They're already calling it the storm of the century—it wouldn't be the first time somebody blew a blizzard out of proportion, but certain things shouldn't be messed around with. This would be one of them. It's always better for people to be cautious than to not take things seriously.

The driveway leading from the main road to the remote cabin is blocked off with yellow tape. All it takes is a quick flash of my badge to roll through and move closer to the scene of who knows how many crimes. I have to dismiss a gentle shiver that runs through me at the thought. Is this where Maddie died? That kind of question isn't going to help anything, but I realize now it's sat at the forefront of my thoughts since finding her image posted on the cabin wall. One of so many others documented for posterity. Only a true maniac does something like that.

A maniac I met and paid no attention to. He got away from me.

I recognize Captain Felch's tall, broad frame at a distance. He lifts a hand and I do the same before parking the car near the many police vehicles scattered around the scene. So many. It seems the entire force and half the FBI are out here working the area, looking for ... anything. Anything that could lead us closer to him.

"How are we feeling today?" the captain asks. I appreciate the question, but what I appreciate more is the offhand way he asks. He doesn't want to make a big deal of what took place out here yesterday, when I all but fell apart for a little while.

"Watching for snow," I tell him.

We both look up at the foreboding sky, and he grunts. "We should get socked. I can smell it in the air." He then grimaces while stretching out his right arm. "And I feel it in my bones. An old injury, it always flares up when there's a storm coming."

"Well, now I believe we're in for it." I jerk my chin toward the cabin, where work lights positioned around its perimeter cast an unnatural glare that matches what's coming from inside the dilapidated structure. But then there's nothing natural about this place or what's inside. "How's it coming along here?"

"They've worked throughout the night. There has been a lot to sift through."

"Did they take down the photos and articles?"

"Negative, though they did document each and every one. But they're dusting for prints, too, so right now, they're being as careful as possible not to disturb the display." Of course, they would be. Now that it's clear this is the den of a killer, it's critical to preserve any evidence or means of identifying the man behind everything.

I follow him inside, pulling on a pair of latex gloves as always. "Really," Felch murmurs, "they shouldn't have been removing anything from the interior yesterday. It was too soon."

He's absolutely right, but at the time, I wasn't interested in right and wrong. I was much too busy reeling from the fact that I recognized the man in one of the photos being removed from the cabin.

"Apparently, your boss down at the field office threw a fit."

That's news to me. I turn to him, arching an eyebrow. "Really? I'm surprised I didn't hear anything about that." Is he leaving me out of the loop?

My silent question is quickly answered by the flush that colors his cheeks. "I think they got word out there that this is a little more personal for you than anyone originally imagined."

Terrific. "I don't want anybody treating me with kid gloves."

"They won't." His lips twitch with barely concealed humor. "I'm sure they know better."

I don't want to be pulled from the case. It's more important than ever to keep my personal feelings separate from the facts. "Do we have any info pulled on this guy's aliases?"

"Funny you should mention that, because I was going to mention it to you that so far, all of the prints found around here match the name he used at the boarding school, on his employment paperwork."

"We know that's got to be fabricated. He wouldn't use his real name." But the prints match.

He answers the question I haven't yet asked. "Nowadays, they can do a lot with prosthetics. I read an article about that recently, as a matter of fact. They're so small, even the professionals running Livescan can't tell the difference."

"You think he was using fake fingerprints," I muse, and something about it feels right. That would explain how he's been able to get away with using a dead man's identity as his own.

He's been at this a long time, after all. I'm sure he knows all the tricks by now. He must have been awfully good even back when he killed my sister.

Don't think about her. But that's the thing. You tell yourself not to think about something, and naturally it's the only thing that comes to mind. It's basic psychology. Considering there's a PhD behind my name, one would think I'd have a better handle on that.

"How's the storm going to affect the search?" I ask as we step into what I've called the trophy room, at least in my own mind. "How are we protecting the integrity of the cabin?"

"Once everything's documented — and that should be completed in a matter of a few hours — they're going to start taking things offsite, down to the station. We've already cleared room for the boxes." Naturally, extra care will have to be taken to preserve the integrity of the evidence, since any small detail could make or break the case. No one can afford to be careless or clumsy.

I can't help the way my gaze is drawn to the article about Maddie. Articles, plural, I realize as I move closer to the wall. The captain stands behind me, silent, allowing me to get a closer look once again. I wasn't exactly in the right frame of mind to do any reading yesterday. Seeing her picture along with so many others was more than enough to throw me into a tailspin.

He documented her well. There are the articles published when she was first missing, the ones that described her discovery and identification. The headlines may as well be chapter headings in the book that is my family history. *Girl, 15, Missing ... A Tragic Conclusion ... A Family In Tatters.*

"We're sorry, Mr. and Mrs. Forrest, but the body has been identified as belonging to Madeline."

"He was proud of himself," I muse aloud, staring at the wall. I can't help but imagine him standing here, staring at these very images and the words written about her. About what he had wrought.

"They normally are, especially when they're not caught.' I hear the frustration in the captain's voice, and I can certainly relate. "But one thing at a time. I know this brings everything to the forefront for you."

I shake my head firmly and pull my gaze away from the reminders of my family's pain and loss. "You might be surprised how close it always is to the forefront," I admit. "Even before I came here."

I turn in a slow circle, noting again the number of articles and images and how they overlap for lack of space to adequately cover all of his many crimes. "How many? Has anybody counted?"

He clears his throat behind me. "Thirteen."

My stomach clenches around the delicious, well-intentioned breakfast Mitch treated me to. Thirteen.

That means there're another twelve families represented here. I wonder if any of them managed to stay together in the face of their tragedy. I wonder if they go to sleep at night wondering whether the person who took their daughter, sister, best friend away will ever face justice.

I need to get out of here. I can't look at this anymore. The captain follows without question, though I almost wish he wouldn't. I get the feeling he thinks he needs to look after me, and while I appreciate it, I've never liked being babied. If I could find the words, I would tell him I've learned to live with the pain. Having it thrown in my face like this is difficult, but I'll get through it.

"Until we can attach him to any of these crimes," the captain points out, "we can't guarantee he's the person who killed your sister."

"I understand that." I pull in a deep breath, welcoming the way the cold makes my lungs burn. It clears my head. It grounds me. And when I'm thinking clearly, I can remind myself he's right. Yes, assuming this monster is behind Maddie's murder is the most logical conclusion, but there's no fact behind it. Nothing we can really go on besides the certainty deep in my gut that I've exchanged words with the man who blew my life apart.

You thought Ed Schiff kidnapped Camille, too. Yes, that seemed like the most likely conclusion, as well. But

Ed Schiff didn't have a room full of clippings, either. Or a long, red braid pinned up beside the image of a girl with the same hair.

He's about to say something probably intended to spare my feelings when his phone rings. "This is Felch," he says, and it doesn't take a heartbeat before his brows knit together. "Slow down. Say that again?"

He holds the phone away from his ear and presses the speaker button so I can hear the voice on the other end. "The call just came in. A family from out in Bangor staying in some cabins down by the lake. A little boy went missing while he was sledding and the parents are frantic. They can't find him anywhere."

We exchange a silent look that needs no explanation.

A missing boy in the middle of the woods.

And here we are, facing down a blizzard coming closer every minute.

3

"hat do we know?" the captain asks while the wheels start turning in my head. Another missing child. Is this a coincidence?

"The kid is nine years old, staying in an Airbnb with his family and some friends. He went sledding, the mom says. She said he was out there for fifteen minutes and when she went to call him in, all she found was his sled at the bottom of the hill."

"How long ago was this?" I ask.

"She said it was around eleven o'clock."

So around forty minutes ago. "Send me the address," the captain barks on his way to his car. I look at him, my eyebrows raised, and he waves me on. I hustle to my car and follow him, away from the cabin and down to Lake Morgan.

A nine year old boy. I have to ask myself if our mystery man is behind this. Would he still be in the area, for one thing? Or is he three states away, congratulating himself for getting away with yet another vicious crime? Laughing at me for letting him slip through my fingers?

Thinking back on those clippings, I have my doubts. It doesn't fit his MO. He goes for young girls, not little boys. Still, there's a prickle along the back of my neck as I follow the captain to the other end of town, where tourists have long rented cabins. Normally, they do so in the spring and summer, and maybe the early fall—leaf peepers, mostly, in September and October. I wasn't aware there were so many people renting cabins for vacations at this time of year. Bed-and-breakfasts, sure, but when there's no way of knowing what the weather will bring, it seems like a bit of a risk. Nobody wants to be stuck in an unfamiliar, remote location when snow is about to fall.

The area is gorgeous, and once we arrive, I can understand the appeal. The snowy woods are something out of a Robert Frost poem, and smoke rises from the chimneys of snow-capped roofs. Cabins line the lakeside and I'm sure, once darkness begins to fall, nothing in the world would look as appealing as the light glowing from behind the windows.

I pull in behind the captain, and before we've even stepped foot on the ground, a woman in her mid-thirties with eyes that are already raw from weeping propels herself onto the porch.

"Please, help us! He still isn't back!" A man steps up behind her and wraps his arms around her waist before she turns to him and buries her face against his chest, twisting his sweater in her fists.

"We're going to do our best," Captain Felch promises as we approach. It's getting colder by the minute. *He's only nine years old.*

"Why don't we go inside?" I suggest. "My name is Alexis Forrest, I work with the FBI." I'm not sure what compels me to take the lead, but the captain says nothing to stop me. "Captain Felch is with the local police."

Inside the cabin, there are two other couples and a handful of children. Two of them look to be around the age of the missing boy, and both of them wear a haunted, wide-eyed look I can identify with. I was only a year older when we got word Maddie was missing.

"I'm Rob Duncan. This is my wife, Krista." Rob scrubs a hand over his short, sandy hair before releasing a choked sob. "I have to get out there. I have to get out there!"

The captain places a hand on the man's shoulder when it looks like he's about to bolt outside and maybe freeze to death. "We're going to get officers out there looking for your boy, sir. You have my word on that."

"Can you tell us what happened?" I ask, eyeing the others. It's not a large cabin—certainly big enough for a small family, but the room is pretty cramped with all the extra bodies hovering around.

"Kris?" One of the other two women touches Krista's shoulder. "We'll take the kids over to our cabin for now. Just to give you guys a little room. But we'll be right over there, okay?" Krista's head bobs up and down and fresh tears soak into her turtleneck before she wipes her cheeks with trembling hands.

Once the cabin clears out a little, Rob offers me a look at his phone. "Cayden," he tells me. It's a photo of a gap-toothed little boy with his mother's brown eyes and his father's sandy hair, proudly holding up a sled emblazoned with the Teenage Mutant Ninja Turtles. Before I have the chance to ask, he says, "This was taken a week ago. We got him that sled for this trip. Can you believe it? He couldn't wait to take it out."

"Can you give us an idea of the timeline" the captain asks, looking to Krista. She sinks onto a plaid sofa and holds her head in her hands, whimpering.

"I told him, I'm going to set a timer on my phone for fifteen minutes. And while he was out there, I would fix a snack." She lets out a broken, choked laugh. "He worked up an appetite out there, you know? He couldn't wait for lunch."

"And who were the people who were just here, in the cabin? Family?" Captain Felch asks.

Rob shakes his head. "Friends of ours. They're staying in the next two cabins."

"And were the kids out there with Cayden?" I ask.

Krista's head swings back-and-forth. "He wanted to go back out by himself. Just fifteen more minutes," she whispers before covering her face. "Why did I let him go? Why didn't I tell him to stay? Where could he have gone?" Her pain is thick, intense. I watch helplessly as her husband sits beside her and gathers her in his arms, murmuring what little comfort he can offer. At a time like this, it's not easy to know what to say.

"It's not your fault," I hear him whisper, and I see the anguish on his face that only deepens when she shakes her head. She can't let herself believe it.

The captain pulls me aside. "Find out what you can from the other families," he murmurs. "Anything they saw. I'll stay here with them and get a description to put out on the wire."

The story Krista told is easily corroborated by her friends, all of whom are clustered in the next cabin over. At a time like this, I guess they don't want to be apart in case they hear something. "Is Cayden going to be okay?" one of the older kids asks me after I introduce myself.

I sink into a crouch and hold his gaze when I smile. "We're gonna do our best. I promise." Not the answer he wanted to hear, but it's the only honest answer there is.

One of the women gathers the kids together. "Why don't you guys put on the TV for a while, and we'll talk to this nice lady." She's trying her best. I hear the fear in her voice and notice the way she strokes the hair of the little guy in front of me before letting him go. He must be one of hers.

The adults wander into the kitchen, which is more modern than I would expect from such a rustic looking place. Then again, I'm sure there's only so far some vacationers want to go when it comes to roughing it. I, for one, appreciate little comforts like the shiny espresso maker sitting on the counter.

The woman who spoke to the kids shakes my hand. "Monica Nolan. My husband, Greg. And this is Beth and Jake Foster."

Beth shakes my hand before pressing her lips together in a tight line. "My Bryce and her Connor are in Cayden's class," she explains.

"So you're all out here together?"

Greg nods. I catch the way he keeps looking out into the living room, like he's making sure the kids are there. "Yeah, we figured we'd rent a cabin out here for a long weekend. The kids wanted to play in the snow, we wanted to get a little relaxation."

"And you're all friends through school?" Their heads bob up and down. "And can you tell me what happened today?"

Monica draws her hands inside her sleeves before wrapping her arms around herself. "The kids went out after breakfast while we, you know, had our coffee and chatted. The men took turns watching them."

"Exactly where were they sledding?"

Jake waves me over to a window overlooking a hill that slopes downward from the cabins and ends maybe twenty or thirty feet from the road. "We figured it was perfect for them. Right where we could keep our eyes on them. Me and Greg were out there with them at first, then Rob took a turn before we went back out. We came in later to get some coffee and warm up."

"But we were watching them all the time," Monica insists. "And it was only another twenty minutes or so before we told them to all come in. I was afraid they were going to lose toes out there if they spent too much longer."

"But Cayden wanted to stay out," I murmur.

"I'm sure Krista was watching from the kitchen the whole time." Beth's face crumbles with emotion. "It's not like Cayden to wander off."

"That's true," Monica agrees. "We always joke he was born an old man. He is the most trustworthy little guy."

It seems like trustworthy children are disappearing right and left lately. The thought chills my blood. "Did you happen to hear a car pass at any point? Voices?"

"No." Beth leans against her husband, and tears fill her eyes. "Trust me. I've been asking myself that question for the past hour." The four of them are haunted, stricken, swaying slightly under the weight of guilt and dread.

"I'm going to head out and take a look at the scene. I'll let you know if we have any other questions or updates, alright?" I notice as I'm heading out that the kids don't seem particularly interested in the cartoons they're watching. Not the older ones, at least. Their sisters are a little younger, and might not quite understand what's going on, but the boys do.

Captain Felch is still with the Duncan family, and I return to their cabin in time to hear him giving them his best assurance that we'll do everything in our power to find their boy. Krista's broken sobs tug at my heart. At a time like this, the impulse to offer empty assurances is almost too much to resist. I can't stand seeing and hearing this woman fall apart without wanting to give her a little comfort. There's no comfort to be offered, at least not yet.

And certainly none that she would accept unless it had to do with finding her boy safe and well.

4

"I can't just sit around here." Rob rubs his hands over his pant legs, then shakes them out like there's too much nervous energy flowing through his trim, athletic body. He has to get rid of it somehow. "I'm not going to sit here while my boy is out there somewhere, needing me."

"I understand how terrible this is—"

The sharp look he gives me cuts off the rest of the comfort I was trying to offer. "Do you have children?"

It's clear where this is going. "No, sir," I murmur.

"Then with all due respect, you don't understand. You could work a hundred cases like this, and you'll never understand." His bloodshot eyes burn with anger I know doesn't belong to me. It was stirred to life by whoever took his son away. I only happen to be in the room.

The captain steps up behind me. "I, for one, do have children of my own. And I do understand how terrible it is, sitting back when there's nothing you can do. My daughter had a burst appendix nearly two years ago, and if I could have gone in there and picked up a scalpel, I would have. I had to sit and feel helpless while strangers worked on her. It was hell. I'm sure it's worse for you, with so many questions."

He goes to Rob and touches his shoulder, squeezing hard. "But you're not from around here. I wouldn't even let locals search these words alone. It would be too easy to get lost, and there's a blizzard on the way."

"Oh, no!" Krista lets out a pained sob. "The storm! I forgot the storm."

"We'll have people out there looking for him as long as it's prudent." The captain looks my way, and I see the concern and sadness in his eyes. The timing couldn't possibly be worse.

"What about animals?" It's clear the distressed father is grasping at straws, trying his hardest to wrap his head around the unthinkable. "Maybe something came along and attacked? Maybe he had to run away?"

"Anything is possible. We don't want to rule anything out yet." Though truly, I have to wonder. From the vantage point of the rear window, I didn't make out so much as a drop of blood on the snow.

"He didn't scream." I turn to Krista, who is curled up on the couch with her arms wrapped around her middle and her knees drawn close to her chest. "He didn't make a sound. He would have screamed if there were something scary out there."

"You don't know that," Rob insisted. Panic ran through his words and the energy in the cabin was turning thicker, more charged.

You don't know anything happened! She probably stopped off at a friend's house on the way home. That was Mom's refrain the night Maddie first vanished. She didn't want to face the truth, and I don't blame her. She needed to believe there was a simple explanation,

"We're going to go out and take a look at the area," the captain tells him. "And it would be for the best if only Agent Forrest and myself went out there. Let's try to keep things as close to the way they were while Cayden was down there as possible. Stay here," he insists in a gentle but firm voice I know is meant only for Rob.

"But …"

"Mr. Duncan. Either I'm going to have my people out there searching for your boy, or I'll have half of them searching for him and half of them searching for you. Now, you tell me. Which would you rather?" That question seems to be the pin that pops the balloon of Rob Duncan's panic. His shoulders drop and his face falls once there's nothing to do but face reality. He is powerless here.

"We'll be back," I promise before heading on to the porch. This area must have seemed beautiful and welcoming when the families first arrived. Now? I can imagine it looks pretty bleak. Not to mention endless, with miles of bare trees stretching in all directions.

Once the captain joins me, we set off for the slope behind the cabins, trudging through untouched snow. "What's your first impression?" he asks once we're out of earshot of the cabin and the couple inside.

"Not good," I admit as we carefully make our way down the hill. It's slippery, perfect for sledding. I'm sure the kids were thrilled. I, for one, will consider myself lucky if I make it down without twisting or breaking anything.

"Yes, the same here. It's startling how little time it takes for something like this to happen. You think you understand. All your training tells you how quickly things can change."

"But knowing it and seeing it are two different things," I conclude.

"Exactly."

It's a relief when we reach the bottom of the hill, then begin surveying the scene. It's clear from the number of small footprints where the kids chose to go up and down the hill. There are larger prints, too, likely from the men. They go up and down, as well, and I can imagine how tired they must have felt after helping the kids all morning. Children have boundless energy, but even the healthiest adult can't keep up indefinitely.

"Well, this is disheartening." The captain stands with his hands on his hips, shaking his head as he looks toward the road. "Tell me what you don't see."

I lift my head, frowning. "What do you mean? I don't follow."

A grim smile tugs at the corners of his mouth. "Usually, you're five steps ahead of me. Either I'm getting sharper or lack of sleep is catching up with you."

Considering where I woke up this morning and the scant number of hours that had passed since I drifted off to sleep in Mitch's arms, he might be on to something. "No comment," I tell him with a sigh.

"The footprints. There's something missing."

It's like a challenge I need to rise to. What is he seeing that I've missed? I study the footprints, especially the set leading away from the base of the slope. Small footprints, left by a child.

That's when it hits me. "There aren't any prints but his." My head snaps up and I look left, then right, before crossing the quiet road to check out the snow on the other side. Aside from a few prints that might have been left by deer, it's pristine. Untouched.

"There you go. I knew you would catch it."

Our eyes meet across the road. "Meaning someone drove up and convinced him to get in the car. There was no struggle, he wasn't grabbed. He was enticed."

"It isn't difficult to entice a child if you use the right words." He removes his uniform hat and scrubs a hand over his neat, salt and pepper hair before plopping it back on his head. "A missing dog. That's usually all it takes."

Yes, and a sweet, helpful kid—the way Cayden has been described—would want to help. It would make him a hero, wouldn't it? Helping a stranger find a lost pet or something similar. Sometimes, that's all it takes. And all Krista would have to do is look down at a cutting board or turn away to refill her coffee, and that would be it.

We trudge back up the hill to our vehicles, where the captain uses his radio. "We need to issue an all-points bulletin," he announces. "And let's set a press conference an hour from now. We need to get word out to the public, and ASAP. There's a nine-year-old boy missing, and the clock is ticking."

In more ways than one. The clouds are piling up, and it won't be long before the flakes start to fall. The way it's been described, it's the sort of storm that could block the roads for days. I don't want to imagine the toll that would take on the family. If that were my boy out there, I wouldn't care much about the snow or the danger. I would want everyone to put everything into searching for him.

The captain finishes rattling off a description of Cayden, then turns back to me. "We have a problem."

"And here I was, thinking about how easy everything's been so far."

"We've already got half our manpower out around town, making sure everything's in place before the storm hits. That doesn't leave much bandwidth for asking questions around here."

"I'm more than happy to help."

His lips twitch with the beginnings of a wry grin. "I thought you would be."

5

My breath comes out in a thick cloud once I step up onto the small porch that wraps halfway around the quaint cabin in hopes of viewing the layout of the property. Scanning the area, I count seven cabins in all — including the one whose porch I'm standing on, stomping my feet to keep them warm in the increasingly frigid temperatures. It's like Mother Nature herself feels the need to remind me of the time constraints. The clock is ticking louder than ever.

Four of the cabins are smaller, like this one. Having already taken a look around inside, I know there is one bedroom in these small models. The larger models feature a second story beneath a peaked roof, and it appears as though half of the cabins fit that description.

And from the looks of it, most of them are in use. Smoke rises from the chimneys, blown by the wind that seems to pick up in intensity every time I step back outside. I shudder to imagine it getting much worse, though it is supposed to.

The three cabins in which Cayden's family and their friends stayed in are clustered closer together, and I imagine that's why these three particular cabins were chosen for this trip. The others are spread out along the banks of the small, man-made lake. There's a path that runs around the lake's perimeter, which I assume is meant for strolling, bike riding, and the like. It hasn't been shoveled since the last snow, but it has been put to use by multiple people whose footprints have turned to ice. It's safer to walk in the snow rather than take my chances. No one would ever mistake me for an ice skater.

It comes as a relief when, upon knocking on the door of the first cabin I come to, a sweet-faced middle-aged woman peers out from behind the curtain over the window set in the wood. When I raise my badge—a silent signal, the sort of thing that crosses language barriers—she opens the door an inch or two before pulling her thick, zippered hoodie tightly closed. "Can I help you?" she asks in a soft but tight voice. Apprehensive. I can't imagine how she would feel otherwise at my sudden appearance.

"My name is Alexis Forrest, and I'm here with local police to investigate a child's disappearance this morning."

The fine lines already etched at the corners of her eyes and bracketing her mouth deepen. "So that's what all the commotion was about. Oh, that's terrible." She cranes her neck, peering around the door frame and peering over toward where the Duncan cabin sits. "I heard someone calling out a name."

"Cayden," I offer.

"Yes, that's it. How awful." She shivers, then throws an apologetic look my way. "I'm sorry," she murmurs, then holds the door open wider. "Please, come in. You must be half frozen. Can I offer you something hot to drink?"

"No, thank you. I do appreciate it, though." This is one of the smaller cabins, laid out exactly the same as the others I have seen today. It's also very neatly kept. There are personal touches, too, like a handful of black-and-white photos displayed on the mantel over the fireplace. Interesting. That's not typical in a vacation rental. "Are you here alone?" I ask.

Her head bobs up and down while she reaches for a remote control to turn down the volume on the TV. "Yeah, it's just me."

"A little weekend getaway? How unfortunate, since we're supposed to get snowed in."

"Oh, no. I'm not here on vacation." She uses a scrunchie around her wrist to pull back shoulder length blonde hair streaked with gray. "I rented the cabin for the winter. That's how most of the cabins are run. There're only a few for vacationers. The rest are long-term rentals."

I make a note of this. It explains her personal touches. "How long have you been here?"

"A few weeks. I have a little more than two months to go, and I might end up having to extend it if I can. Please, have a seat." She gestures toward an armchair positioned close to the sofa, both of which are near enough a cheerful little fire that the heat begins seeping into my muscles by the time I've settled in the chair.

"This is very cozy," I observe with a smile as I strip off my fleece-lined gloves and hold my hands out toward the fire. "I can think of worse ways to spend the winter."

She doesn't look quite so enthusiastic. "Well, it's less expensive than my old apartment."

When I raise my eyebrows, she shrugs and her gaze darts away from mine almost like she wishes she hadn't said it. "I'm going through a break-up, and I couldn't afford the rent on my own. I got evicted last month."

"I'm sorry to hear that. Did you live in Broken Hill?"

"The past ten years. I work over at a gas station in town. This is my day off. And here I was, thinking it would be peaceful."

"I'm very sorry to disturb you. I know if I had a day off, I wouldn't want to deal with a stranger asking questions."

She shakes her head adamantly, and the lines at the corners of her eyes deepen when she narrows them. "Oh, no. There are much worse things than that. Like searching for your missing kid. A boy, I take it?"

"Nine years old. Short, sandy blonde hair and freckles. He was wearing a puffy, blue coat."

"I'll certainly keep an eye out for him around here." She folds her arms and shakes her head. "You just never know. When we were kids, we were always taught to avoid strangers and that sort of thing, but when you're that little and you don't know any better, and a grown up seems nice ..."

"Exactly."

"Do you think that's what happened here?"

"I can't say." And not only because we aren't certain of exactly how Cayden was taken. The fewer details I offer at this stage, the better. Word travels fast, and as kind as this woman seems, she could be the town gossip for all I know. Or involved with kidnapping.

I clear my throat and poise the pen over my notepad. "So, you say you've been here for a few weeks. Have you seen anything ... Noteworthy? Unusual?"

Right away, she chuckles, and my breath catches. "Oh, that's a word for it."

"How so?"

"Now, I see all sorts of people in my line of work. People passing through, people sneaking around, trying to ask for change from drivers coming in for gas or snacks. And I don't judge." She holds up a pair of weathered hands. "I don't. Because you never know what a person has gone through. I mean, here I am, evicted and everything. I never thought something like that would happen to me. I was only able to take what I could fit in my car, not that I had all that much to begin with."

She sits up a little straighter after having trailed off. "But some of those people on the other side of the lake?" She blows out a sigh and rolls her eyes.

"What about them?"

"Partying all the time. All hours of the day and night. Especially the night," she adds with a cynical laugh.

"Are all of the cabins occupied, do you know?"

"As far as I know. This is the only time of day when there's any peace and quiet around here. They're probably sleeping it off."

"They're that loud, that they keep you up?"

"Oh, only when they decide to fight."

I'm starting to get an idea of the sort of people she's talking about. "Domestic?"

"I do hear women screaming," she confirms with a nod. "But it's more like bickering. Not like, you know." She winces before mouthing the word *abuse*.

Then she continues, "But sometimes it's men yelling at each other. One night, a man was practically shrieking about having something stolen from him. I got the feeling he was talking about drugs, but I wasn't about to head over to ask. You have to understand, I normally would. When it sounds like someone is upset or needs help, I don't like to sit back and pretend I don't hear them."

"But something stops you when it comes to them?"

She shivers and shakes her head. "They don't seem like the sort of people you want to approach. I figured, what if they're all messed up on whatever they're smoking or shooting and decide to come over here and take everything I have? It's not much to begin with."

"Being on your own, I can see how that would be a concern. It's generally a good idea to stay out of situations like that."

"I thought so." She sounds relieved, like she feels better now that she's been absolved. "Anyhow, there's always different people coming and going. From what I understand, they rent by the week."

"Gotcha." I make note of that as well, then stand. "I don't want to take up any more of your time."

"Not at all." She groans on standing. "Except for the people I run into at work, you're the only person I've spoken to lately. It's sort of nice, and a big change from all the yelling and fighting."

I give her my card, which only features my name and cell number. "If you can think of anything else — something you might have seen today, anything odd after I've left — feel free to give me a call. And be careful with this storm coming. Do you have enough supplies to get you through?"

"It's sweet of you to ask. Yes, I made sure I stocked up at the store after I got off work yesterday." Now that I glance toward the kitchen, I see the cereal boxes, instant coffee, canned tuna and soup stacked up on the counter.

This is not what I expected to find. I suppose it's a good business move, to an extent. But renting by the week to people with sketchy intentions can only backfire in the end. I'm not sure I'd want to risk damage to my property, but what do I know? I'm not a landlord.

I have to wonder if the families currently waiting with their hearts in their throats have any idea of the sort of activity that goes on so close to where they chose to take their vacation. Something tells me they don't, or they would have mentioned it by now. I know that would be my first guess if anything happened to my son. But they never spoke of it.

I begin walking beside the ice-covered path, heading for the trio of cabins across the lake. The odds of finding Cayden in any of them are slim.

But I'm going to keep an eye out for him, just in case.

6

It doesn't come as a surprise, the silence that answers me once I've knocked on the door of the first cabin I come to. I'm on the far side of the property now, and this is one of the structures whose chimney is not belching smoke. I knock again, listening hard.

Silence.

There's a late model Chevy parked beneath the branches of the towering spruce—one of the tail lights is broken, and the passenger side window has been replaced by a garbage bag taped to the frame. It gives me a fairly decent impression of who I would find inside the cabin if they were awake and sober enough to answer.

I continue to the next cabin sitting roughly a hundred yards from the first. Instead of a Chevy, I find what might at one time have been a pretty sharp looking Beretta. It's seen better days. At first glance, I'd be surprised if it started, but those older cars were built to last. Not so much nowadays. Empty bottles and cans litter the porch, while a ceramic bowl used as an ashtray overflows with butts.

Once again, when I knock, there's no sound from inside. I'm starting to think this was a waste of time. It's probably way too early for any of these people to be up if they party the way the woman across the lake described. From what I'm seeing, I have no reason to believe otherwise. And I can't wait too long, because I'm racing the storm. I wouldn't want to be stuck out here when it starts to come down heavy.

By the time I reach the third cabin, this is looking more like an exercise in futility, but I knock on the door anyway and hope for the best.

This time, I hear faint, shuffling footsteps coming from inside. There's a curtain covering the window beside the door and it shifts slightly to the side. Once again I raise my badge—and that might not have been the best move, since the single eye peering at me goes so wide, it bulges. "There's a missing kid. I'm only investigating his disappearance."

Finally, the door opens, and immediately the odor of old food and cigarette smoke hits me in the face. "Sorry. You kind of freaked me out."

She might be in her mid-twenties, or she could be forty. That's how thin and drawn and unhealthy she looks. She tucks stringy brown hair behind her ears and licks her chapped lips before asking, "You sure you're not here to search something? Because you know you can't do that without a warrant, right? This is private property."

What a conclusion to jump to. I guess if I were in her shoes, I would be this defensive. "Like I said, a little boy went missing this morning. From the cabin over there." I've almost rounded the lake by now, and the trio of cabins Cayden and his family and friends stayed in are close enough to be easily seen from where we stand. I point in that direction. "He was out sledding, and then he vanished."

"Oh. One of those kids? Just today? That's wild."

"Why do you say that?"

Rather than let me inside, she joins me on the porch, casting a worried look inside before closing the door. Intuition tells me she doesn't want to wake up whoever else is in there. She shoves her hands into the front pocket of her hoodie, which her very thin body swims in. "I heard them over there. I saw them."

Yes, part of the hill is visible from here. "Can you tell me what you saw or heard?"

"Well, they weren't being quiet, you know?" She lets out a shaky laugh that exposes the terrible state her teeth are in. "They were screaming and having fun. I don't sleep too well anyway, so they woke me up."

"Did you interact with them at all?"

"Oh, no. I didn't even come outside. I'm not, like, a Karen. I used to have fun when I was a kid, too. But then they must have stopped, because it got quiet. I went back to sleep. I didn't wake up until you knocked on the door."

Once again, so close, but so far away. I was hoping she could tell me something. The description of a car, anything. I might not trust her if she was high, but she seems sober as she fishes a pack of cigarettes and a lighter from her pocket. Sober and straightforward.

"How long have you been staying here?"

She gives me a skeptical look, arching a thin eyebrow. "Why?"

"I'm only curious as to what you've seen around here. How familiar you are with the area. Whether you've seen any shady characters around."

That might have been the wrong choice of words. She blurts out a laugh before taking a pull from her cigarette. "Yeah. Shady. I see lots of those."

"You know what I mean. Do you know of anybody around here who, you know, maybe likes kids a little too much? Maybe they watch them a little too close? That sort of thing."

Her drawn face twists into an expression of disgust. "No, nothing like that."

"But have you been here long?"

She exhales sharply before nodding her head. "I don't know how much longer. I can't afford this place anymore."

"How come? If you don't mind my asking."

She lifts a thin shoulder like it doesn't matter. "Back when I first started coming here, it was three-fifty a week. That's no joke, either, but usually I can split it. Now?"

Her laughter is as cold as the air around us. "Some new company bought all the cabins early this fall and started renting them out on Airbnb."

"I've been hearing a lot of horror stories about people who rent out properties on that site."

"Right, because it drives out all the locals. Nobody can afford it. Now, the new company wants seven hundred a week."

I blow out a surprised whistle. "That's pretty steep."

"Sure, and they want people who can afford it. People coming here for vacations. Forget people who just need a place to live." She flicks ash from her glowing tip then shakes her head. "I mean, I've got evictions on my record. I can't get an apartment. This was my only option, and they're taking it away because they're greedy. But who cares, right? All that matters is the almighty dollar."

"I can't imagine how stressful that must be."

She side-eyes me, keeping her thoughts to herself, but the smirk on her chapped lips tells me all I need to know about what she's thinking. "Anyway, that's that. I have until the end of next week to figure out what I'm going to do. And now, we're supposed to get slammed by all this snow. Maybe that'll buy me a few more days. But who knows?"

"Do you know the name of the company that owns the cabins?"

"Yeah, hang on. I have it somewhere inside." She finishes her smoke and stubs out the butt with the heel of her worn out clog slipper before turning toward the door. Something stops her, though, and she gives me a furtive look while reaching for the doorknob. "Um, you should wait here."

"I'm not here about anything you may or may not be doing in that cabin."

"Yeah, but still ..."

I hold up my hands to show I'm no threat before she opens the door. From where I'm standing, I can see half of the living room and kitchen area, and it's about as cluttered and filthy as I would guess. But there's nothing inside to give any indication of Cayden's presence, and there are no new tire prints in the thin layer of snow that fell between the midnight hour and this morning. The car hasn't left, and there are no fresh footprints other than mine. Nobody has been in or out of this place in hours.

"Here you go. I knew there was this letter here, talking about the price increase." She picks up an envelope from a small table just inside the doorway and hands it to me. Inside there is a sheet of paper whose letterhead reads White Oak Vacation Rentals.

"Thank you very much. I appreciate your time. Please, don't hesitate to call if you see or hear anything you think might help."

I hand her one of my cards and she takes it, but her soft snort paired with yet another smirk tells me my chances aren't great. "Yeah, no offense, but we don't trust cops around here."

Message received.

7

By the time I return to the Duncans' cabin, I know I'm not imagining things. It has gotten markedly colder and windier since I first arrived with the captain. I duck into my car and start the engine for the sake of warming up in front of the vents. The digital readout on the dash confirms the temperature is a good twenty degrees colder than it was hours ago. It's only going to get worse.

And there's a kid out there somewhere.

A gust of wind rocks the car slightly and I gasp in surprise at the intensity while waiting for a page to load on my phone. White Oak Vacation Rentals. Something about the stories I've heard this morning has worked its way under my skin. What happened today may have nothing at all to do with the practices of whoever owns the company, but I'm curious about them anyway. There are people being pushed out of the only temporary home they can afford, and while I can understand wanting to attract a more dependable and reliable clientele who are less likely to warrant a call to the police, doubling the weekly rent is a big move. I hope they don't think they're going to snap up properties all over Broken Hill.

It looks like they already have plenty of properties in the area according to the splashy website. The images are the type I expected to find, laughing couples, happy families, gorgeous, panoramic vistas. I pull up the menu and tap the *Our Properties* tab, which takes me to a page featuring a lengthy list broken down by state. They aren't only in Maine, but also well established in Vermont, New Hampshire, Connecticut, and in Massachusetts. So far, it seems they haven't gotten a foothold in Broken Hill aside from the cabins here at the lake. But how much longer will it be?

The site also features links to the company's various social media accounts. I head to their Instagram page, where there are even more enticing, colorful images like the ones on the website.

Along with a large number of comments from people following the account. And most of them are less than glowing. I tap one of the posts featuring a property in New Hampshire and scroll through the dozens of responses.

We used to rent here every summer, now it's three times the price.

What are people supposed to do when they want to rent a house now? And you're eating up all the residential properties.

This company is a scam!!! I worked for them. They're evil. Do not rent with them!

I wonder what they did to deserve that kind of scathing comment. Granted, that could have come from an angry ex-employee after being fired. That sort of thing needs to be taken with a grain of salt.

But the more I scroll through, it seems like White Oak has earned more than its share of detractors. It reminds me of something Dad used to tell me when I was a kid. If one person complains about something you do, that's their problem. If everybody does, it's your problem. And the more I explore, the more convinced I am that White Oak is the problem. No, nothing they're doing is illegal, per se. But a business practice doesn't have to be illegal to be crummy.

I have to wonder if a company like this—so big, widespread—would mount security cameras anywhere on the property. That would make sense, especially considering some of the less-than-savory activity that clearly takes place on the other side of the lake. From where I'm seated, it doesn't look as though there's anything attached to the outside of the structure, but I can only see part of the cabin from here.

It feels like taking my life in my hands by stepping out of the car again but I force myself through it, clutching the top of my coat and the bottom of my hood tight in my gloved fists to ward off as much of the icy wind as I can while I check out the cabin's exterior. My heart sinks when I find nothing that vaguely resembles a camera. So much for that idea.

Krista looks at me with so much hope and dread mixed together when she answers the door at my knock. "Excuse me, Mrs. Duncan."

"Do you know anything?"

"I'm sorry, not yet." Her face falls as the little bit of hope she dared entertain drains away. "Actually, I was hoping I could use your bathroom. If you wouldn't mind." I've been out here for hours now.

"Oh. Not at all." She backs up, allowing me inside. Rob stands at the kitchen window, gazing out. Unmoving. Blaming himself, no doubt. If only there were a way to soothe that kind of pain, but I don't know of any such method. And it's all too familiar. Many was the day I watched my father stare exactly the way Rob is now.

The bathroom is just beyond the kitchen, tucked in the back corner of the cabin. Not very large, but then the necessities are covered. I can easily span the room's dimensions by outstretching my arms. I wonder if this cabin was renovated somehow once White Oak took over. I'm not exactly sure why the company has me intrigued. I doubt there's any connection to Cayden's disappearance, which has to be my focal point. Otherwise, I need to track down Lila's killer—and possibly Maddie's.

Focal points aside, something is off about the entire situation around here. I can't put my finger on it, but the fact that it lingers in the back of my mind says my gut picked up on something I may not yet have processed. If there's one thing I can trust, it's my gut. Alright, so maybe I wasn't quite correct about Ed Schiff. He didn't kidnap Camille Martin. But he wasn't innocent, either, and now he's awaiting trial before going to prison for a long time.

What am I missing here? Why was I compelled to research the company when I should have been researching something related to Cayden?

Once I finished washing my hands, I return to the couple. The silence in the cabin is profound, and I almost regret having to clear my throat and break it. "Unrelated, but something caught my attention as I was questioning the other people staying in the cabins around the lake. You rented for the weekend through White Oak vacation rentals, I assume?"

Rob turns around, blinking like he's surprised. "Yeah, that's the company name. Do you think they had something to do with this?"

"Like I said, I doubt it's related in any way. But I understand the company owns a lot of other properties in New England, and they recently purchased these cabins to be used for vacationers rather than renting to locals, as they normally do."

Krista snorts softly. "I don't think those people across the lake are here on vacation."

"I did speak to one of them," I confirm. "For what it's worth, I don't think they have anything to do with Cayden's disappearance. Most of them are still sleeping it off, to be blunt. And I didn't see any signs of anyone coming or going since the snow fell overnight."

"I was wondering about that," Rob admits. "I didn't want to make assumptions, but ..."

"Anyway, I found it curious and wondered whether you noticed anything ... off. The way they do business, I mean."

I know when they both tip their head to the side almost in unison that I'm barking up the wrong tree. I wouldn't be surprised if they both wonder why I care—or why I would ask that at a time like this.

Because I can't bear their confused stares, I look away, my gaze drifting up toward what have to be brand new cabinets in the kitchen. It seems like the property was flipped recently—that would explain the shiny new counters and the little amenities like the espresso maker.

It might explain something else, as well. "What is that?" I take a few slow steps into the kitchen, staring up at the corner where the cabinet meets the wall, close to the window.

"What's what?" Rob joins me, and I point to the small, round something or other that appears to be mounted in the corner, close to the ceiling.

I was looking for cameras, wasn't I? I didn't expect them to be inside the cabins.

"I never noticed that before." I look at him in time to see him waving Krista into the room. She drags her feet, and I'm sure she wonders why it matters. I'm sure I would, too.

Until she sees it, and her hands drop to her sides. "That looks like a camera. Is that a camera?"

I look around, then grab one of the wooden chairs positioned around a small, round table and pull it up to the counter, then climb on to get a better look.

"That is exactly what it is," I whisper. Who's looking at me right now?

"Oh, you have to be kidding!" Krista falls back, gasping in horror, while I hop from the chair and start searching the rest of the cabin. I look up into the corners, near the ceiling, and my heart sinks when I spot not one but two small lenses in opposite corners of the bedroom.

And by the time I return to the bathroom, my stomach is churning. Rob stands in the doorway and the two of us scan the ceiling, the walls, everything. "There it is." I hate having to do this, but I point to the corner above the bathtub. "I guess I don't need to ask if you knew about this."

His already pallid complexion goes white as a sheet of paper. "You mean ... somebody's been watching us? In here?" He can't take his eyes from that camera, and I'm sure his head is reeling at the implications.

"It looks that way."

As if they needed another layer of horror added to what's already been a horrible day.

And outside the window, the first flakes of snow are beginning to come down.

8

"I just showered there this morning!" Krista rubs her arms briskly, her mouth wide open in horror. "Why did we ever come here? We should have stayed home!"

I can't pretend I wouldn't think along the same lines if I were her.

"What if somebody's been watching all this time and they knew we were in here while Cayden was outside?" It's the ranting of a terrified parent, I'm sure, but I don't want to shut Rob's questions down out of hand. It's important to keep him as calm as I can.

"I will certainly look at that as a possibility." The fact is, I can't tell how this ties in or whether it ties in at all. But if it hadn't been for Cayden's disappearance, who's to say how long it would have taken someone to find out they've been recorded throughout their stay?

"Oh, I feel so dirty." Krista rakes her fingers through her chestnut hair before gasping. "What about the other cabins? Beth and Monica."

"Let me handle this." The last thing we need is Krista making phone calls and spreading panic. "We're going to get to the bottom of it, I promise you."

"Cayden matters more right now," Rob insists.

"And we already have people out there looking for your son." I'm already halfway out the door, jogging over to the next cabin.

The families have split up, I notice on arrival. "We figured the kids could use a nap," Monica explains. "Though I wonder if the older ones will get much sleep. But it's already been a long day."

Because I don't know whether there's audio capability on the cameras, I hold a finger to my lips before motioning for her to follow me. Whoever set things up must have decided to stick with what worked, because sure enough, there is a camera mounted in the same position in the kitchen. I peer briefly into the bathroom to confirm that camera's presence, as well. "Is your husband here?"

Forest of Shadows

She shakes her head. "He's with Beth and Jake. What's going on?"

"And the kids are in the second bedroom?" Her head bobs up and down, her eyes darting over my face. I can only imagine how I must be scaring her. "Come with me." I head to the porch and she follows, shivering in the cold air once we're outside.

"What is this all about?"

"Completely by accident, I discovered the presence of cameras in the Duncans' cabin. So far, I've found two in your cabin—kitchen and bathroom, the same location."

Her reaction is the same as Krista's. Immediately, she wraps her arms around herself and goes pale. "Someone's watching us?"

"I don't mean to upset everybody when there's already so much going on, but you deserve to know, and to do what you want with that information."

"Well I sure don't want to stay here!" Then she looks toward the Duncan cabin and winces. "But they won't want to leave, will they?"

"I can't imagine they would. You might be able to find something in town, but I would advise moving fast."

"I don't know what to do." She holds her head in her hands, distraught. "It wouldn't feel right, leaving with Cayden missing. But how do we stay? I'm certainly never going to use that bathroom."

"You may be able to disable the cameras," I suggest. "It's private property, sure, but I doubt there's any court anywhere that would prosecute If you broke them. Covering them with tape would probably be easier."

"But who's to say there aren't more?" Our eyes meet and I know she's right. I wouldn't get a wink of sleep until I tore the cabin apart, making sure I hadn't missed a hidden camera.

We both watch as a small, late model sedan rolls up and parks between the two cabins. "You know who that is?" I murmur, watching intently.

"No, we only got in yesterday." And it isn't anyone from the force, for sure.

A middle-aged woman climbs out from behind the wheel. "Housekeeping," she announces with a smile and a wave before reaching into her back seat and pulling out a bucket full of cleaning supplies.

I looked toward Monica, who nods in understanding. "Right, housekeeping services were included in the rental."

All at once, the front door to the Duncans' cabin flies open, and Krista races down the front steps. "What is wrong with you people?" she demands, storming toward the housekeeper's car. "You're sick, that's what's wrong! How dare you? How dare you violate people this way? Do you know we'll sue? We will sue every single person who has anything to do with this company!"

It's clear as I run their way that the housekeeper is flustered, lost. "I ... I don't ..."

"Well? What, you didn't think we would find out? How many other people have you recorded? How many other files are there?"

"Krista!" Rob calls out from the porch as I reach the women and step between them since it looks like Krista is ready to throw fists while the housekeeper only sputters in a language I'm unfamiliar with, wide-eyed, her dark skin going darker thanks to the way she flushes in what could be confusion or fear. Probably both.

"No ... understand ..." the woman manages before her eyes fill with tears.

"Oh, I'm sure you understand just fine!" Rob takes hold of his wife in the middle of her tirade, locking his arms around her waist and pulling her back.

"I'll speak with her," I tell him while he takes Krista inside. With the door closed I still hear her ranting. I can't say I blame her even if I get the feeling she's barking up the wrong tree by blaming the woman who washes the floors. But then what do I know? I looked at a maintenance man and saw nothing but a guy doing his job. It never occurred to me he might have a cabin in the woods where he takes his victims.

The woman is shaking when I turn to her, and I doubt it has only to do with the bitter wind and the flakes blowing in our faces. "My name is Agent Forrest, with the FBI."

"FBI?" She falls back a step.

"You're not in any trouble, I promise. A little boy went missing today, and we're looking for him. Those are his parents—they were staying in that cabin." After gesturing in that direction, I ask, "What's your name?"

"Maria."

"Maria, I'm going to ask you a question and I need you to tell me the truth."

"Alright. I'll help in any way I can." When she isn't being screamed at, she has a perfectly good command of English—so long as she's given time to speak slowly. I doubt I would be able to defend myself coherently if I were suddenly accosted by a ranting woman.

"Are you aware of the presence of recording equipment in the cabins?"

No, she wasn't. It's in the way her head snaps back. The way her eyes widened the instant before her head swings back and forth. "No. No, there isn't. There's no such thing. They must be confused."

"Ma'am, I discovered them myself, in this cabin and the next one over. I haven't had the chance to look through any of the others."

"Cameras? Like ... spying ..."

"It's a possibility, yes."

"Oh, no, I didn't know anything." She casts a horrified look in the direction of the Duncans' cabin. "When did they do it?" she murmurs, shaking her head.

"How long have you worked for White Oak Vacation Rentals?"

"I don't."

I tip my head to the side. "But you do clean the cabins?"

"It was Broken Hill Management Services who hired me. The people who used to own the cabins. I've been doing this for many years."

"And this is the first time you've ever heard anything like this?"

"The first time. I still can't believe it."

"So White Oak kept you on after the property changed hands?"

"Yes, yes. Kept me on. No meeting, no phone call, nothing. Just a different name on my paycheck. I figure, they still pay on time, I'll work for them."

"So you don't know any of the people who run the place?"

"No, nobody."

"And how long has it been since they changed hands?"

"I'm not sure. Six months? But they took their time. They redid these cabins first, and now they're going to do the other ones." She looks across the lake, scowling. "I don't clean those. I will once they empty out."

The snow is picking up, going from heavy flurries to something more substantial. "I'm sorry, I'm not trying to hold you up from your work," I offer. "I know you'll be in a hurry to get out of here before things get much worse."

"Maybe I will skip that cabin today." She eyes the Duncan cabin warily, and I can't say I blame her. I wouldn't want to go in there, either, wondering if someone would attack.

There are a pair of uniformed officers a few hundred feet down the path I made it a point to avoid earlier, and I wave them over to me, meeting them halfway with my fists shoved deep in my pockets. It wasn't supposed to start this early—Mitch said early evening, and it's barely late afternoon. I only hope it stays like this for a while. It's freezing, it's snowing, but it's manageable.

"Keep an eye out for cameras," I tell them after giving them a brief rundown of what I found. "Take a look at the exteriors of the properties you come across. Those cabins," I continue, gesturing toward the ones I visited earlier, where all the parties take place, "might not have any at all, since they haven't been renovated yet. There could still be some on the exterior, though." And if there are, that means we could get a look at whoever drove up and took Cayden. What the property owners did was unforgivable, but there may be a thin silver lining in all of this.

To think I figured I would spend time at the other cabin today. What I've come to think of as Maddie's cabin, since we are still unsure of the name of the man who used it.

Andrew Flynn—whether or not that's his name, he is who I want to look for.

Ever since I first arrived in town, it's been his actions I've focused on.

His crimes.

Was he behind this?

I dismissed him earlier, at least to myself, and I'm still not convinced he stayed in town, much less that he would take a chance like this with a victim who doesn't fit his usual profile. None of the pictures in his trophy room were of boys. They were all girls in their early to mid-teens, at least from my memories of what I found there.

Like Maddie. All these years, did that man walk through life knowing he got away with taking her from us? If it really was him, who messed up? Who was asleep at the wheel and arrested the wrong man? Did they even try to find the truth, or did they go with the easiest, most likely scenario?

So long as I'm pulled into other investigations like this one, I'll never know.

A strong, extended blast of icy wind rocks me back on my heels and reminds me of how little time we have before what is currently a nuisance turns into something far more dangerous.

9

"I don't understand. The roads are still drivable."

Captain Felch pinches the bridge of his nose, wincing. "Alexis, respectfully, when I give an order I expect it to be followed. And that goes for you, too."

"But—"

"No buts." I follow him into his office, anyway, because I'm flabbergasted at his sudden announcement. He wants everybody to come in from their searching, go home if possible, and get some rest.

"Sir, please. It's not undrivable out there yet."

"Yet." The word comes out as sharp as the crack of a whip, so sharp I fall back a step. "And that could change in a heartbeat. I am not going to risk the safety of anyone on this force, nor would I risk yours. I'm telling you. That's enough for today. You won't do anyone any favors if you get yourself wrecked out there, or stranded."

This is unbelievable. There's still at least another hour we could spend searching for Cayden. "The Duncans are counting on us. Cayden is counting on us."

"And like I told Mr. Duncan earlier, I can't split my team in half because somebody decided to go out searching in a bad situation. Even if you knew those woods like the back of your hand, Agent Forrest, all bets are off during a blizzard. Do you know how easy it is for a person to get turned around and to completely lose track of their surroundings? It happens like that." He snaps his fingers, then shakes his head. "I will not be responsible for your safety or anyone else's. Go home. Wait this out. You already have enough going on without risking your neck."

I have never dealt well with being dressed down. Even when I was a kid, even when I deserved it. Leaving my library book at home when I was supposed to bring it to school. Forgetting my homework, being scolded for not doing my best on an exam. Even something as low stakes as drinking the last of the milk without giving anyone the heads up that we were out.

Needless to say, the stakes are much higher now, upping the intensity of my reaction. Frustration builds in my head like the storm building outside. "I'm going to keep looking for another hour."

"Can I take you somewhere and lock you inside?" he asks as he shrugs into his heavy coat. "Maybe to your mother's house?"

"I can handle it."

"Famous last words." He heaves a sigh while wrapping a scarf around his neck. "I know there's nothing I can say to stop you, so I'm going to stop wasting my breath. If you're going out, go now, while the roads are clear. But please, don't push it."

"I won't."

"Forgive me if I don't quite believe you."

I'm as determined as possible as I stride through the station. That determination gets knocked back by the wind that threatens to push me further into the building as soon as I've opened the door. Maybe he's right. Maybe I need to call it a night. Mitch is waiting for me, after all.

Still, I reason as I fight my way to the car that when we made our plans, the snow wasn't supposed to start falling until roughly this time. There are already several inches of fresh snow on the sidewalk in front of the station and what's coming down is blowing nearly sideways thanks to the relentless wind. I have to wonder if any of the businesses on Main Street are even open at this point.

When I get to the car, I fire off a quick message. **I'm going to drive for an hour to search for the little boy who went missing today, but I'll meet you at the house later? Figured the restaurant would be closed anyway.**

The car's heater has barely kicked in when my phone rings. "I promise, I won't be long," I tell Mitch upon answering.

"I would feel a lot better if you would leave the searching until the storm moves out."

"I know, but—"

"No buts." This would not be the right time to comment on how sexy he sounds when he's stern, so I keep it to myself. "Now, I know better than to think you'll do anything I suggest, but I want it on the record that I don't feel good about the idea of you being out there in this. There's a reason I closed the store early and headed home."

"I'm glad you did."

"I'm also in the middle of fixing dinner for us."

"You're making me feel pretty bad."

"Am I?" He sighs. "I didn't mean to. But I did want to let you know that I'm here, waiting."

"And you have no idea how much that means." I check the clock on the dash. "It's barely seven now. I can still make our date, even if we aren't going to the restaurant. Would that work?"

"Sure. The lasagna will keep warm. But please, I'm begging you, be careful out there."

In the rearview mirror, I scan the street behind me. "There's hardly anybody out. It'll just be me, anyway."

"And did you ever think there's a reason nobody's out there?"

"I'll be careful." Because that's a lot safer than reminding him of what I do for a living and that there are people counting on me. Krista Duncan is still in that cabin, hoping and praying her only child is found safe and healthy. I can't let her down. I at least want to be able to look her in the eye and tell her I did everything I could.

And right now, doing everything I can means pulling out of this lot and setting off for the roads surrounding the woods. For the sake of safety, I'll stick to Route 1 and the wider, two-lane roads branching off from it. I know better than to venture through the woods themselves, where time and countless cars have worn crisscrossing paths over the years. I might be taking a risk, but I'm not suicidal.

I'm barely two blocks from the station when it becomes clear my wipers aren't doing a great job even at full power. No sooner do they sweep across the windshield than a fresh onslaught of flakes nearly blinds me. But the roads themselves are in good condition after a few coatings of brine and a layer of salt, so I keep moving, using the high beams to navigate.

What do I hope to find? I don't know. A sign, something, anything. I found Camille Martin by the side of the road, barely breathing and nearly frozen solid. It was a complete accident, a case of being in the right place at the right time. There's never any telling what might happen.

Cayden was wearing a bright blue, puffy coat. That's what I keep watching for as I drive along and try to ignore the way the wind tries to push the car into the next lane.

The high beams illuminate a damaged tree yards ahead. Fresh damage, too—a large gash has been taken out of the trunk at roughly the height of a truck, something higher off the ground than my Corolla.

I slow, then stop a few feet from the tree, scanning the area in search of the vehicle that did the damage.

There are no tail lights blazing in the woods, no headlights on the snow. It doesn't look like the vehicle ran off the road in that direction, but there is more damage to smaller trees further away from where I parked. Like the truck or SUV or whatever it was cut a path through them. The wind has turned the tire tracks to little more than slight dips in the snow, but they're visible.

Someone out there could need help.

I park the car, which rocks in the wind and leaves me less than enthusiastic about climbing out. My flashlight waits in the passenger seat and I turn it on to make sure it's working. Then, just in case, I pull my gun from the holster and flip off the safety. I don't know why, but instinct is telling me to be prepared.

The snow is falling thick and heavy and by the time I begin trudging through, it's halfway up my calves. At least I'm dressed for it, but there's only so long before I start to freeze up. The flashlight's strong beam makes it easy to avoid walking straight into a tree, at least, but I'm huffing and puffing by the time I spot fresh footprints ahead of me.

Someone is out here.

"Hello?" The wind picks up my voice and carries it away as soon as it's out of my mouth. I turn in a circle, realizing to my dismay I've wandered far enough from the road that I can no longer see the car. "Hello!" Again, pointless, but I have to try.

My voice may be carried away with the wind, but the sound of an exploding branch only a few feet from my head is certainly loud enough. It takes a second for me to realize the wood did not spontaneously explode. It was a bullet.

All at once, my training kicks in, and I dive behind that same tree for cover with my heart in my throat. I am not searching for a victim lost in the storm. I'm searching for someone who doesn't want to be found.

I peer around the tree in time to spot a dark figure. Tall, bulky, their face covered in thick winter gear. He freezes when my flashlight finds him and I take the opportunity to return fire, but either the adrenaline coursing through my veins or the wind takes the bullet off course. He turns and begins to run, kicking up snow behind him as he stumbles.

And what can I do? The only thing instinct compels me to do.

I run after him.

10

There is nothing in the world but blinding snow and howling wind that almost drowns out the heavy thud of my heart and the rush of blood in my ears. I see him up ahead, a shapeless, dark figure getting smaller all the time. Sheer instinct pushes me forward while good sense tells me to stop. It's instinct that wins out, instinct and certainty. He has to be stopped. I have to stop him.

And not only because he took a shot at me. Though that's part of what pushes me forward. He has a gun, he fired on me, which means he feels threatened.

Which means he's done something to feel threatened over.

But when I stumble and fall in snow that reaches my shoulders once I've thrown my hands in front of me to catch my fall, it takes too long to get up. Exhaustion hasn't just crept in. It's slammed into me, pulling me under. I lift my head, but it's no use—I can't see anything but wind driven snow that's caked onto my hood and my eyelashes and even my face. A face I can barely feel in this relentless, icy wind. I pull in as deep a breath as I can once I find my way to my feet. The air is so cold it burns my lungs and leaves me gasping in pain.

And I am completely turned around.

No. No, this didn't happen. I am not completely lost in the woods, in the snow, unable to see and with no idea where the car is. Where the road is. Where anything is.

Yet there's no denying the facts, either. And this moment, the fact is, I could freeze to death out here while the man I was chasing is now nowhere to be found. Mitch is waiting for me, and I'm going to freeze to death. They're going to find me here once the storm is over and the snow begins to thaw. And I won't be any help to anyone.

I don't know what finally soaks into my frozen brain, but something snaps me out of the panic threatening to end my life. I can't stay here, freaking out and freezing.

I look down to where I fell—already, the snow is shifting and new flakes are filling in the indent my body left behind, but it's clear the direction my body was moving in when I went down. I do a full hundred-eighty-degree turn and head in a straight line away from that place, hoping there's some sense in this theory and that my new course will take me back to the road. It's all I have now. My only hope.

The wind is at my back, one small blessing in the middle of so much frozen disaster. It helps push me, keeps me moving, and it keeps the worst of the snowfall out of my face. I use my gloves to brush the caked snow from my hood, but it's quickly covered again. My legs are heavier with every plodding step and my feet don't feel like they're attached to my body anymore. Move, move! I will not let my mother lose another child. I will not let Mitch or Captain Felch blame themselves for letting me come out here tonight. Yes, there's a possible killer out there somewhere, getting away from me yet again. Whoever he is, he'll have to wait. I have to live through this. There's no other option.

My flashlight's normally strong beam is weak but still effective, lighting my way as I stumble clumsily through so much frozen blankness. Snow has a way of wiping out all hope of identifying anything, and every tree looks the same.

I push forward because there's no choice, though every heavy, exhausting step leads me closer to nothing. I could be walking deeper into the woods for all I know. The mental image of a grim Felch knocking on Mom's front door is all that keeps me going. She cannot go through that again. Neither can Dad. I need to get out of this.

At first, I'm sure I'm seeing things. A flash of color that stands out in the flashlight's beam. I do my best to wipe the snow from my face so I can see clearly — it's still there, up ahead.

And it's bright blue.

"Cayden!" A fresh burst of adrenaline courses is its way through my veins. I don't feel the cold anymore. I don't hear the wind. I only hear my voice rising above all of it. "Cayden!"

It's him, he's here, his little body still wrapped in his blue coat and propped against a tree. He's half covered in snow — I caught his arm and his hood, the only two things clearly visible now that he is half-buried.

"Cayden, please." I doubt he could hear me if he were conscious, which he is not. His eyes are closed, his face deathly white.

And soaking into his raised hood is a splash of red. Blood. He's bleeding from his head.

Instantly, all of my training comes back. You don't move a body, but then I don't know if he's dead or alive yet. I touch my fingers to his neck, but naturally, I can't feel anything through my heavy glove. I grab one of the fingers in my teeth and pull, exposing my skin to the bitter cold before touching his neck again. Come on, come on. Let me feel something. But no matter how hard I wish or hope or demand, the result is the same. There's nothing. It could be my half-frozen fingers or sheer dread leaving me unable to process a pulse. I pray that's all it is.

One thing is for sure, I can't leave him here. Alive or dead, there's no way. I couldn't guarantee we could find him again, for one thing. And even if he's gone, I won't leave him behind. Even if I don't have the first idea how to get back to the road. And I was having a difficult enough time before there was someone to carry.

"Come on, Cayden. Come on, pal. We'll get you out of here." He's limp and so, so cold. I can't afford to cry. Not now. I can only move, stumbling worse than ever, falling against one trunk after another when my feet betray me and leave me stumbling. My strength was already flagging, but now it's verging on nonexistent even with adrenaline and desperation in the mix. I don't know how much longer I can do this. Every breath takes effort, every time I lift my foot to bring it down again. Deep, so deep, the snow. My muscles are burning, and I can barely see a few feet in front of me.

All at once, it's there. A break in the trees. The wind shifts direction, and for a split second, everything clears before going white again.

But it's enough to give me a glimpse of the road up ahead.

And it gives me new energy, even with the wind now blowing in my face again. I duck my head and push forward with Cayden's face—so cold—against my neck. Is my body heat enough to help him? Does it matter now? I still don't know if he's dead or alive.

I stumble out onto the road, which is now snow covered. All the brine in the world can only do so much against a storm this intense. Why didn't I leave the lights on so I could find it when I came back? That's easy. I didn't think I'd go that far, and I was in a hurry. There will be plenty of time to berate myself later.

I don't find the car. I stumble over it. It's the driver's side headlight – I clip it with my thigh and go down on one knee, but any bit of nuisance pain that results is outweighed by relief. "I've got you, just stay with me," I beg. Pushing myself to my feet, I stumble to the driver's side door and fight to open it when the wind tries to blow it shut.

A minute later, we're together in the front seat. I start the engine and could weep with joy when the heat starts pumping into the enclosed space. Even without it, just being out of the howling wind is a relief.

"It's alright, buddy. I've got you. You're going to be alright." But I don't know that, do I? Because, as I bundle his limp body into the passenger seat, there's still no movement. No pulse. Not even the fluttering of his eyelids.

But he could be revived. There has to be something they can do for him. I need to believe that as I fumble through my pocket for my phone, willing my half-frozen fingers to work while steering with the other hand. Whoever was left at the station sounds fatigued and impatient when they answer the phone.

"This is Forrest!" I bark. "I found Cayden Duncan in the woods and I'm on my way to the hospital. I can't find a pulse and I don't know how long he was out there. He has a head wound. I can't find a pulse. They need to be ready." I'm rambling, repeating myself, fighting back exhausted, helpless tears.

He has to live. He has to.

11

Will I ever be warm again?

My hands close tighter around a paper cup full of steaming, hot coffee. I can't feel it. Yes, I know it's hot. If I take a sip, it burns my tongue a little. But my hands are still so cold. The sort of cold that settles in a person's bones for good.

I'm used to the station being full of voices. Ringing phones. The opening and closing of drawers, the squeak of chairs, coughing and clearing of throats. With today's crew being roughly a quarter of what it normally is, there's an unnatural silence, instead. The few who managed to make it in work quietly, while others are outside now, helping locate stranded motorists, assessing storm damage, helping with clean-up where they can. The snow didn't quit dumping down until it was nearly dawn. Now, a few hours later, there's nothing but the occasional weak flurry. In twelve hours, two feet fell, though the drifts are five and six feet high against some of the buildings in town.

I noticed that on my way from the hospital.

I lift the cup to my lips and inhale the steam rising from the surface of the coffee before taking a sip. The scalding hot liquid is a stark contrast to the cold so severe it makes me shiver. Even while I sit beside a radiator, with Captain Felch's coat draped over my shoulders since my own coat has still not dried out.

The coat's owner sighs as he returns to his office. I look up to find his sorrowful expression and know what he's going to say before he utters a word. "The Duncans finally made it to the hospital. We had to send the plow out to the lake to clear the road for them."

"I wanted to be there when they arrived."

"Alexis." He lowers himself into his desk chair with a sigh. "You've already done everything you could. There was nothing to be gained from being there when the Duncans arrived."

I disagree, but I know better than to think he'll understand.

"You did everything you could." He speaks slowly, deliberately, staring at me with an intensity that makes me uncomfortable. I look down at the coffee, biting my tongue. He doesn't know. He wasn't there.

And he didn't have to hear the doctor's final assessment mere minutes after making it to the hospital. "I'm sorry, but he's gone."

"He was already deceased when you found him," the captain reminds me. "You did your best. You did better than any of us. You also came close to losing your own life. You could have died out there the way he did. You gave everything to find that boy, and you did, and …"

"What? Now they have a body to take home to Bangor? Is that what you were going to say?"

"If it were up to me, you would have stayed at the hospital."

That's startling. It snaps me out of my funk, if only momentarily. "Excuse me?"

"You were half-frozen and in shock when you arrived, according to the staff I spoke with. You should have stayed and let them assess you."

"I'm fine."

"You realize that simply saying those words doesn't magically make it so." When I groan, he raps his knuckles against the desk, startling me into sitting upright. "Listen to me. You're a good agent. Excellent, even. You're devoted and determined.

Forest of Shadows

You also take far too many risks with your life, and you seem to forget you are only human. Flesh and blood. You're not The Terminator, Agent Forrest."

Something about the reference makes me crack a smile. "I really am alright," I insist, but gentler this time. "I'm not going to fall apart or anything. I was so close to that man, though. I have to believe it was he who left Cayden there, meaning he is the reason Cayden ended up dead. Nothing else makes any sense. Why would he be out there in the middle of a blizzard? Why would he fire on me?"

"You have sustained more throughout your short stay here in town than anyone else on the force. More than anyone I've ever seen, and I graduated from the academy when you were in diapers. But everyone has their limits."

The worst part is, deep down inside—beyond my ego, beyond my disappointment and my impotent rage — I know he's right. The mind can only handle so much before it starts to break. And I'm carrying so very many questions and disappointments and frustrations.

"He could've killed you." The captain grimaces when our eyes meet. "Is that what you want me to say? Is that what you need to hear to finally get through to you? You could have been killed last night, if not by the storm, then by the gunman. It's time for you to take care of yourself."

"What are you driving at?"

"I'm driving at you taking time off."

"That can't happen."

"But it is going to happen, because I said so."

"Do you think it's that simple? Just because you said so? I'm here to do a job." And he isn't my boss, but I bite my tongue rather than remind him. It would sound too childish.

"Yes, and Camille Martin is alive and well thanks to you. At least, physically. I have no doubt it will take a lot of time and a therapist help to get her through the rest."

"I'm sure you're right about that."

"Why does she deserve professional help, but you don't?"

He thinks he's very clever, boxing me in like this. "Because I am a professional, too. I know what I have to do."

"We both know it's not that simple, Alexis. You don't see surgeons operating on themselves, do you?"

This is getting me nowhere. Either I'm too exhausted to come up with a coherent argument, or he's making sense. "Fine. I will speak to a therapist."

"Good. I'm glad to hear it."

"Later."

"Now, wait a minute—"

"There's no time for me to take off. There just isn't. There's too much to be done."

"Such as what? Cayden Duncan is now in the custody of the medical examiner, preparing the body for release to the family."

"And what were we working on before the call came in to say Cayden was missing?"

"There's only so much you can do on your own. There is a ton of evidence to sift through. The cabin is buried at the moment, so anything left behind won't be processed until we can get the plows out there. Considering we are already plowing half the town, it's going to take time."

"Alright. Then I'll look into whoever it was behind the cameras in the Duncan's cabin. Somebody's out there recording people without their consent. I want to find out who was behind that."

He rubs a knuckle against the spot where his eyebrows nearly meet over the bridge of his nose. "You have me at a loss. Why are you so determined to grind yourself down like this?"

"Who said I am?"

"Agent, you were involved in a shootout last night. That is very real, and there is a protocol to follow after such an event. Pretend to ignore that all you want, but I'm not going to let this go. And if I need to go over your head and speak to your boss about this, I will. I won't like it, but I'll do it if it means getting you the help you deserve."

It's clear I am wasting my breath. "I promise. I will speak to a therapist. But I cannot take the time off. I'll stick to asking questions for now, how about that? I'll lay low."

He only sighs before leaning back in his chair. "See, that's the thing. You can try to lay low all you want, but somehow you manage to find trouble."

"Is that my fault?" It's an honest question.

"No—but I need you to remember you don't have to do everything alone. Alright? Can you at least admit you don't need to do everything on your own?"

"Sure. I can admit that."

"Why do I feel like that's all I'll get you to admit?"

Because it is. "I thought I would start at Broken Hill Management. They're the company that originally owned the properties before White Oak took over. I want to confirm those cameras weren't already there before the property changed hands."

"Well, I doubt anyone will be in the office today. Do me a favor and at least wait until tomorrow. Take the rest of today for yourself. Get some rest. I know you haven't slept." He's right about that, but it doesn't take much of a guesser to figure it out. He met me at the hospital and followed me here. I had the dubious pleasure of watching the sunrise this morning, giving me a look at the storm's damage.

I stand slowly, groaning softly as my tight, sore muscles alert me to their unhappiness. I can't forget how I put my body through the ringer last night. "I'll get some sleep."

"I'm glad to hear it. Are you okay to drive?"

"Sure. I don't have far to go."

"Alexis?" I pause, looking over my shoulder. "You did everything you could. You went above and beyond. That poor kid would have been buried out there for who knows how long, and the family would have suffered needlessly. You're a hero, even if you did take too much of a risk."

"Thanks." A hero. I certainly don't feel like one.

If anything, I'm more determined than ever to dig deeper. If I couldn't find Cayden in time to save his life, I can at least uncover who made those families feel exposed and violated in those cabins.

Which means I will make a pitstop at the management company if they're open. Forget waiting. It's not like I would get any rest, anyway. Not when the memory of holding that little boy's body close to mine is still so fresh. So painful.

12

Broken Hill Management Services sits in a row of commercial buildings off of Main Street, two blocks down from Mitch's bookstore. The store is closed now, as planned. I still haven't spoken to Mitch outside of explaining why I missed dinner last night—he seemed to understand, but I heard the disappointment in his voice. I wish there were a way to explain my devotion to the job, and how when I'm in the middle of something like the Cayden Duncan case, I can't drop everything … even if it means dropping someone I care very much about, instead.

Someone always has to lose out. In the end, it usually ends up being me. Because I certainly would have rather spent the night eating and laughing and cuddling with Mitch than being shot at and trudging my way through knee-deep snow. I'll have to find a way to make it up to him, and not because I think he expects me to. In fact, the opposite is true. He understands. He always has. Still, he means too much to me to let him fall by the wayside. I'm not going to make that mistake again. Not when life is so much better with him in it than it is when he's not there.

Right now, however, I steer the Corolla into a freshly plowed lot that sits behind the row of buildings and is accessible via a narrow alley. The snow that's been pushed off to both sides of the alley makes it even more narrow, but I manage to squeak through with inches to spare before entering the lot. Mine is one of four cars total—I doubt many people felt it necessary to fight their way into work this morning. With all the warning we had prior to the storm, they had time to make other plans.

The lights are on in the management building, though. The door is unlocked, too. A bell chimes softly before I step inside, grateful for the warmth that is so delicious on a day like this. The air would be cold enough on its own, but add a couple of feet of snow for it to blow across and I'm surprised my breath doesn't freeze in front of my face before entering the heated office.

"Broken Hill Property Management, please hold." There is a single employee sitting at one of four desks arranged in the small office. She cradles the receiver of a landline phone between her ear and her shoulder while typing rapidly on her keyboard. "Broken Hill Property Management, please hold."

I lift a gloved hand to let her know there's no rush before scanning the framed photos on the walls. Properties the company owns, I realize. They must not have thought to take down an image of the cabins at the lake. But the property did only recently change hands, after all. I suppose they haven't had the chance.

It's five minutes or so before the frazzled girl hangs up the phone. Her sigh is soft, heavy with fatigue, before she looks at me. "Please, tell me you're not here to complain about being snowed in at one of our properties."

Considering I'm standing in front of her, there's little chance of this visit involving being snowed in. Does she think I walked all this way? "I'm not here for that." But the sight of my badge doesn't soothe her any. In fact, she stiffens, eyes widening, nostrils flaring. Funny how that happens. One look at the badge and suddenly, people start questioning everything they've ever done.

"Who are you? Why did you come here?" she asks in a voice that's suddenly higher in pitch. Stress response. Right on schedule.

"I'm not here to cause trouble, I promise."

"Then why are you here? Why would the FBI be in town? Why come here?"

"Please, believe me. I'm not the enemy. I'm not here to arrest you or anything. I only have a few questions about one of your properties out on Lake Morgan."

"Oh." Her eyelids flutter and I'm fairly sure the breath she takes is the first one she's taken since she saw the badge. Then her head snaps back. "Wait. We don't own that property anymore. That is, everything's been finalized, and White Oak has already done work inside, and—"

"I'm aware of some of that. I spoke yesterday with a housekeeper hired by your company who has been kept on by White Oak. She was the one who pointed me in this direction."

Suspicion sweeps over her face, darkening her expression for an instant. "Who was it?"

We are getting way off track. "Why don't we start again?" I suggest. "My name is Alexis Forrest. I grew up here in Broken Hill, and I originally came in for the Camille Martin disappearance."

She gasps in recognition, and I get the feeling I've eased some of her worries if only by briefly distracting her. "What a miracle she was found like she was. I can't tell you how we prayed for her in church."

"Your prayers helped, I'm sure." I approach her cluttered desk and extend a hand. "It's nice to meet you, Miss…"

"Carver. Lisa."

"Lisa." She's young, maybe a little younger than me, but there's a wariness about her that tells me she still has suspicions. She suspects the reason I'm here will end in trouble for her boss. I see it in the way she keeps moistening her lips with her tongue, I feel it in the clamminess of her palm when we shake hands. There's something fishy going on around here. If she were some innocent kid working in an office, she might be a little freaked at the presence of an FBI agent, but if she had nothing to worry about …?

The phone rings, and she rolls her eyes. "It seems like it's pretty busy around here today, Lisa."

"Just give me one second, please. I'm the only one who managed to make it in, and all of our guests have a million questions and complaints this morning."

Yes, and according to what I hear on my side of the conversation, it seems someone is complaining about being snowed in. "Yes, ma'am. We've arranged with the plowing company to get out there as soon as possible, but there's something of a waiting list at the moment. There are only two trucks and a lot of ground to cover."

She ends the call with a sigh. "Sorry about that. It's been like this all morning."

"I can only imagine. I won't take up too much more of your time, I promise, but I do have questions about that property by the lake. A little boy was kidnapped behind the cabins yesterday morning. Unfortunately, when he was located, he ..."

I swallow hard and push past the emotion that tightened my throat to a pinhole. "He didn't make it."

Lisa gasps, touching a hand to her chest. "No. That's terrible! Wait, I think I saw the press conference. Um... something Duncan?"

"Yes, unfortunately. That's the one." Her eyes go wide and teary, and a flash of inspiration hits me all at once. "Can I please look through the footage from the cameras on the property?"

It's a gamble, assuming the presence of cameras outside the cabins, but the idea is to remove the possibility of her feigning ignorance. The fact is, I still don't know for sure whether such cameras exist—as far as I know, none were located by the officers I tasked with searching yesterday. The captain sent everybody home shortly after that. I have no idea if anything was found.

Sometimes, you have to fake it. It's as simple as that.

"I'm not sure I understand." But something about the way she won't meet my gaze tells me otherwise.

"The boy was sledding behind one of the cabins and was kidnapped. My hope is, there's footage of the car the kidnapper was driving."

"Oh. I see." Her teeth sink into her lip, and it's all I can do not to jump over the desk and shake her.

"Somebody killed a little boy yesterday," I whisper. "And I have to find him. So please, I need your help."

Her eyes shift to a door leading further back into the building. A back office, one probably belonging to her boss. "I don't know if I'm allowed to do that."

Bingo. She didn't say there was no footage. Only that she's not sure she's allowed to show it to me. "This is an active investigation, Lisa. I have to get a look at this guy, and you might be my only shot at that."

"But ... I should ask my boss ..."

"And if your boss has any problems, they are more than welcome to call me." I take a card from my inside coat pocket and slap it on her desk. "Any time, day or night."

She hesitates another moment before nodding. "Okay. Yesterday, you said? Do you know the time?"

My head is buzzing as I take the liberty of rounding her desk and hovering at her side. "He vanished around eleven in the morning, so maybe we should start a few minutes prior."

"This is highly irregular." Yes, and so is getting kidnapped when all you're doing is sledding under the watchful eye of your mother. There's nothing regular about any of this.

"We have cameras set up all around the property." She pulls up a folder, opening it to reveal a series of images I recognize as coming from the property I walked yesterday.

Slowly she cycles through each camera feed before I point to her screen. "There you go. There he is."

"My goodness," she whispers. "There he is."

Yes, there he is. The same feeling I struggled with when I first observed Camille Martin leaving at the end of her shift at the bookstore washes over me now, only it's even more intense because now, I know for sure how the story ends. When it was Camille, there was still so much uncertainty. No way of knowing for sure what had become of her.

If only there were a way to go back. To tell him to go inside, to watch TV while his mother fixed a snack. I want to reach for him and grab him and keep him safe. He was so little, slipping and sliding his way up the hill, before throwing himself onto his sled and flying down until he came to a stop at the base. Unfortunately, he stopped outside the camera's range, but not five seconds pass before he ran back into view, dragging the sled behind him as he fought his way back up the hill.

And he slides back down. We wait. I check the timestamp—two minutes until eleven. I know what's happening, and there's nothing I can do about it. There never is, is there?

"And that's it." I can't take my eyes from the screen. It doesn't matter how I wish for him to come back into the frame. He won't. He never will.

"Are there any cameras that could show me the road running behind those cabins?" She flips through the feeds one at a time, eventually returning to the one we started out watching. I don't want to see that now. I don't want to watch Rob Duncan searching in vain for his little boy.

"I'm sorry. I wish I could be of more help."

"Maybe you can."

The phone rings and she answers without looking. "Broken Hill Property Management. Please hold." She presses a button on the switchboard and replaces the receiver.

"I want to see the footage from inside the cabins now."

Her head snaps up. There are lines etched across her otherwise smooth forehead. "What?"

"Inside the cabins. I want to see it."

"I don't understand. I've already shown you all the feeds I have access to." She turns back to her screen and opens the folder labeled Lake Morgan. "See? All we have is the exterior. Are you saying there are cameras inside?"

"If there weren't, would I be asking about them?"

"I swear. I have no idea what you're talking about. The cameras were installed outside to keep an eye on things, but that's it."

I believe her. But that doesn't change what I found. "Do you know who installed the cameras on the outside?"

"Sure. I'll give you their info." Something tells me what matters most to this girl is getting me out of here. I can't say I mind. If she can't help me, I need to speak to someone who can.

13

A gentle tapping at my bedroom door pulls me out of a dream. An ugly dream, full of swirling snow and icy wind and the sick certainty that I wouldn't survive. A dream full of anguish in the form of a limp body that somehow became heavier with every plodding step through snow which — big surprise — grew deeper every second.

In other words, Mom knocked and woke me up at the right time. "Honey? Dinner will be ready in a few minutes."

"Thank you." At least, I think that's what comes out. It's what I intended to say, at least. There's nothing like a midday nap to turn a person upside down. If it hadn't been for the dinner announcement, I might think it was morning.

Dinner. That means I've been in bed for hours without intending to sleep nearly that long. By the time I reached Mom's after leaving the management office, I was almost too wiped out to make the drive. Like everything slammed into me all at once. Fatigue, Grief. The sense of paddling helplessly in the middle of a stormy sea with nothing to hold onto. All of it pushed me through the front door and into a hot shower before I collapsed into bed.

The captain would be so pleased to know I slept most of the day away. Mom was pleased, too. No, thrilled. There's something nice about that. She was here, waiting, worrying. I doubt she would ever give me grief over spending so much time over at Mitch's house, but her face lit up when I walked in. Sometimes I forget she's here, hoping I'll show up. A few years of chilliness between us make it easy to forget. To become absorbed in my own life and forget about hers.

I hope this dinner isn't supposed to be a formal occasion, since I don't have the wherewithal to change out of my pajamas before exiting the bedroom and crossing the hall to where Mom set the dining room table.

"Oh my goodness." There is an abundance of motherly concern in her eyes when she looks me up and down. "You must've been exhausted."

"I was. I'm still a little groggy." Because what's the point in pretending otherwise? I was exhausted, and heartsick, and as I was reminded earlier today, I am not *The Terminator*. I'm only human.

A human who hasn't eaten a decent meal since before the snow began to fall. It seems like so long ago that I woke up in Mitch's bed and was treated to homemade bread straight from his oven. As much as I wish I were with him now, there's something nice about being here. I think my soul needed this. I guess there's never a time when you're too old to need a visit with your mom.

The aroma of pot roast makes my mouth water and my stomach rumble as I take a seat. "This looks incredible. I hope you didn't go to all this trouble for me."

"It's no trouble. Besides, there's nothing like pot roast and mashed potatoes on a day like this," she muses while hacking into a loaf of aromatic rosemary bread. Unlike Mitch's, I don't think this is homemade, though she did warm it in the oven so a pat of butter melts enticingly as soon as I spread it over a slice.

"I hope you don't mind me making a pig of myself." I'm already reaching for a second slice before she sits.

"Don't be silly. I want you to eat. You're too thin as it is."

"Is there such a thing?" I joke, even if I know there is.

"Deflecting with humor. That's my girl." She gives me a familiar, furtive sort of look as she spreads a napkin over her lap. I know what she's thinking before she ever opens her mouth. There's something to be said for history, for being able to read someone like a book. I can brace myself for it.

"I bet you don't act that way around Mitch. I can't imagine he would want to spend so much time with you if you did."

All I can do is shake my head and wince at her heavy-handed joke. "That was a very clumsy segue."

"Who said anything about a segue? I'm only pointing out the obvious." She practically sniffs the air while buttering a piece of bread. "Goodness gracious. Bite my head off, why don't you?"

"Sure. That had nothing to do with you trying to fit Mitch into the conversation in whatever way you could. You can just come out and ask me about him, you know." *I sincerely hope I don't end up regretting that.*

It takes her all of three seconds to pounce after practically licking her chops. "What is going on with you two? Are you rekindling things? Does it seem serious?"

"Okay, hang on." I shake my head, whistling in amazement. "You are too much."

"You know how much I like him. I always did!"

"Me, too!" I retort, mimicking her tone. "But you'll have to forgive me if I tell you we haven't, like, made any promises."

"Is it so wrong for me to want to see you happy?"

"I never said it was wrong," I remind her as gently as I can. Why was I glad to be here again? I'm already forgetting.

"But you do like him? Things are good between you?"

"Yes. I like him very much, and I always have. But I'm not pretending it'll be as easy as stepping right back into his life and picking up where we left off. There's been a lot of water under the bridge for both of us."

"Does he at least understand how you're so busy all the time? That's very important, you know. Strong relationships have broken up over less than your crazy schedule."

I can't deflect so easily. I hear the truth in her words, and something in me makes a discordant noise like a poorly plucked guitar string. "He understands," I decide before spearing a piece of shredded meat on my fork and dredging it through my potatoes. "He's a very understanding person."

"And he was always so crazy about you," she points out, practically singing the words in a smug, motherly way. "And every time we ran into each other before you came back to town, he asked how you were doing."

"You're starting to embarrass me."

"That's my job. Don't you know that by now?" And the thing is, I'm sure she believes it.

"I don't want you to get the wrong idea, is all."

"And what is the wrong idea, exactly?" She is all innocence, blinking her wide eyes. "I'm sure I have no idea what you're talking about."

"Come on. This is me you're talking to. And I know you are already picking out floral arrangements in your head."

"I am not." When all I do is stare, she hunches her shoulders defensively. "Okay, so what if I was looking at mother of the bride dresses online?"

"This is what I'm talking about."

"It's no crime to dream."

"I know. I just don't want you to be disappointed if things don't go the way you hope they will."

"But what if they do?" she counters. "For once, can we imagine things going exactly the way we want them to? Wouldn't that be nice?" Sometimes I forget how positive she always tried to be. It's easy to forget, considering how many years of utter depression and darkness she suffered through. And how many bottles she emptied.

It would be nice if things turned out exactly the way I wanted them to. I can't pretend otherwise. Still, there's a big part of me that wants to discourage her from all these hopeful plans. And not only because I don't want her feelings to be hurt.

I don't want my feelings to be hurt, either. It's a lot safer to play it cool, to be realistic. I'm not in town to stay. Broken Hill used to be the place where my heart lived. It was my home. Now, my home is in Boston. It's where I live. It's where I belong.

Even if I have no actual friends out there outside of people I socialize with on rare occasions outside of work. They are the only people I know, my coworkers. Even then, I wouldn't exactly call them friends. More like warm acquaintances. And there's certainly no one in my life like Mitch. There's never been anybody like him.

"Darn you." I jab in her general direction with my fork. "You get in my head and you make me think things."

"Am I supposed to apologize for that?"

"It might be nice if you at least considered it."

"It's not going to happen, my dear. I'm never going to stop wanting the best for you, and Mitch is the best. I will go on the record with that."

"Your opinion has been noted."

All at once, her smile fades. "I heard about that little boy. I heard you were the one who brought him to the hospital."

She has such a talent for blindsiding me like that. One minute, we're having an awkward but good spirited conversation about my personal life. Next, she wants to talk about a traumatic event. There's never any preparing myself when it comes to her.

"I really wish you wouldn't take chances like that."

"You sound like Captain Felch."

"What a shame you don't listen to him, then."

"I don't know what you want me to say. I came out of it alright. I'm safe."

"Yes, by some miracle. I'm glad I didn't know you were out there. I doubt I could've taken it."

"Well, that's why I don't tell you every little thing, because I know it would worry you. I didn't want to put that on your shoulders."

"Don't act as though you were doing me any favors, young lady. I have no doubt you rushed out with no regard for your own safety. I doubt you thought about anybody else but that poor child."

"I was thinking about his parents, too."

She swallows hard. "Naturally. Well, you were their angel last night."

I shouldn't snicker, but I can't help myself. "An angel would have found that boy in time to save him."

"An angel gave them closure. They didn't have to wait around for the better part of a month, wondering where their baby is." She lowers her cutlery to the plate and sits back in her chair. She's staring at her food but I don't think that's what she sees. She's looking into the past. Remembering.

And so am I, and those memories lead me to the question I've already asked myself. Should I tell her? What difference would it make if I did?

It might make a lot of difference to a man who could be sitting in prison for something he had no part in. When I look at it that way, sparing Mom's nerves doesn't seem quite as important. I'm not trying to shock her or upset her that's the last thing I want. But in a situation like this, I can't worry about coddling her, either.

That doesn't mean I can't be gentle. She's finally in a good place. She's healthy, busy, working on her sobriety. I don't want to ruin that. That monster already ruined enough when he stole my sister and choked the life out of her.

"There's something I wanted to tell you, but I wanted to wait until I knew a little more. Unfortunately, I'm sort of at a standstill."

"What are you talking about? Is something wrong?"

"It has to do with Camille Martin. Finding the cabin she was kept in."

She doesn't have a clue, gazing at me without so much as a shred of dread or suspicion. I hate to do this. I hate him for making me do it.

"Mom." I clear my throat before sighing. "There's no easy way to say this. At the cabin … There was a wall of photos. News clippings and photos of missing girls. You get the idea." Her head bobs up and down, her eyes never leaving my face. "And some of those articles and photos … they involved Maddie."

14

At first, she only stares blankly after my announcement. I don't know if I've shocked her into stony silence or if she's trying to catch up or what. I wait, watching her carefully for any signs of what may be going on in her head.

Finally, she blinks rapidly before her head jerks back. "I don't understand. Is that supposed to mean something?"

She's going to make me spell it out. I doubt it's because she doesn't understand. The woman is a lot of things, but she is not slow on the uptake. She wants to be sure she's hearing me right. To not jump to the most horrific conclusion. "It means ... if all of those articles and photos are mementos of his crimes ... the man who kidnapped Camille could be the man who killed Maddie."

The walls around her are invisible, but I can practically see them fall into place. She folds her arms. Stern, grim. "Absolutely not. That man is in prison. That's where he belongs, and that's where he's going to stay."

"I understand—"

"No, you do not understand. I know you're brilliant and wonderful, and excellent at what you do, but you do not understand. It was Russell Duffy who killed your sister."

I haven't heard his name in so long. For so long, it was worse than the foulest profanity. The ugliest combination of letters. It meant death. The destruction of something that used to be good and pure and perfect. My sister. My family.

"But Mom," I plead quietly, hoping to keep her calm. "What if it wasn't? What if they got it wrong?"

She's trembling, her chin quivering, her eyes filling with tears. "I don't want to hear this."

"And I understand, I do, don't tell me I don't," I insist when her mouth falls open like that's exactly what she was about to do. "We both lost her. We all did. And believe me, the last thing I ever expected to find in that filthy cabin was my sister's picture and all the articles they published about her and about Dad and all of it." She flinches at the mention of my father, someone I've gone out of my way to avoid mentioning until now.

I force a deep, shaky breath to pull myself back from the edge of my temper. Nothing will be accomplished if I lose it on her. And we've already spent enough time separated by ugly words and unspoken pain.

"So you think that was his ... track record or whatever you want to call it?" She waves a hand, scowling.

"It does look that way. Like he was documenting his crimes. Of course, we have to look into the various cases those articles symbolized and learn the circumstances. But it makes sense. It's textbook."

"Madeline's murder was supposedly textbook, as well. Open and shut." She raps on the table with those last three words. "Some lowlife scumbag kidnaps and holds a little girl for the better part of a month before finally getting rid of her like she was nothing."

The pain. It's bottomless, and all it took was hearing my mother recap it to bring it all back. The endless days and nights. Looking for my sister around every corner. Floating through life— numb, absolutely numb to everything and everyone around me. Bumping into people in school, literally running into them because I wasn't looking where I was going. I can't remember doing homework. Literally, I have no memory of participating at all. How I made it through is a mystery to this day. I'm sure the teachers and administrators at my middle school took pity. Everybody knew thanks to the constant local news reports, articles in the paper, missing posters around town. I was the girl with the missing sister.

Soon, I was the girl from the broken family.

For a while, the only sound in the house is that of creaking pipes and groaning wood. Just how long does it take a house to settle, anyway? I would think after so many years, it would've done all of its settling by now.

"If it wasn't Russell Duffy who did it," she finally murmurs, "then that man has sat in prison all this time while an evil, wretched excuse for a human being was free to kill more girls."

"Yes. That's what it would mean."

"There was supposed to be evidence." There's an almost pleading sound in her voice. But she's begging me to understand. "The investigators were sure. The prosecutor. The jury."

"I know. Believe me, I've sat with this for a couple of days now, and I still can't believe it. But I know what I saw in the cabin. He documented the whole case, even after—" My mouth snaps shut, but not quickly enough.

"Oh, no." She covers her face with her hands and shakes her head hard. "Your father."

"I'm sorry. I should never have—"

"I'm not a child." She lowers her hands, glaring at me through eyes now overflowing with tears. "You are the daughter, I am the mother. I don't need you to shelter me from the truth."

"I didn't mean to insult you." Though no matter what she says, I'm still going to tread lightly. This is her daughter we're talking about. It's never going to be easy for her to talk about it. "But I wasn't trying to upset you, either. This isn't easy to talk about. I didn't want to dredge it all up for you."

"No, you would rather take that on yourself. On your shoulders."

"Is that so wrong?"

She runs a hand under both eyes, groaning. "Sweetheart. You can't take care of everybody all the time. Sometimes you need to have a little faith that the people you care about can handle things on their own."

Sure, and maybe if it hadn't been for losing Maddie, I would have a healthier relationship with situations like this. Maybe I wouldn't carry the constant burden of being the daughter who lived. The one who has to make up for everything the daughter who didn't live was never able to do. For twenty years, I've carried that burden even back before I fully understood, when I was too young to know what to do with my feelings. All I could do was manage everybody else's.

She removes her glasses and wipes them on the hem of her cable knit sweater before putting them back in place. "What are you going to do with this?"

"We have a lot more investigating to do. Like I said, we want to go through the cases, collect facts, see if the theory makes sense. There's still a chance it could just be a case of some sick creep collecting grisly stories."

"But you don't believe that, do you?"

"Honestly?" I shake my head. "I have a feeling."

"I've heard that enough to know you're serious. If there's one thing you've always had going for you besides your brains, it's your instincts."

"Thank you."

She shivers and rubs her arms briskly before getting up to check the window, like she's making sure it's closed. It is, of course – it would be a lot colder in here if it weren't. She needs to get away from the table. She needs to think. No matter what she says, I regret having to bring it up. I'm sure she can't get through a week without remembering every gory, painful detail of what the medical examiner described on the stand during the trial.

Naturally, I wasn't allowed to hear about that at the time. I was too young. But there was no keeping me away from the transcripts once I was in a position to get my hands on them when I got older.

It was a dog walker who practically stumbled over her body in a thicket that was being used by one of the dogs as a toilet. By then, Maddie had already been out in the elements for a few days and decomposition had begun. According to the examiner, she'd only been dead for four to five days at most, meaning her captor had kept her alive for weeks before ending her life. Most of her body had already degraded to the point where it wasn't possible to tell the specifics of what was done to her – animals had been at her, as well, further complicating things. But the bruising around her throat was still visible. That's how he killed her. It's how he killed Lila, too.

If. If it was the same man. I have to be careful even in my own head not to jump to conclusions, no matter how likely those conclusions seem.

"I only wanted to make sure you knew in case word gets out," I tell her.

She turns around with a sigh. "Do you think it will? Who would talk?"

"To be honest with you, I don't know, but I want to be careful. I thought you should hear it from me."

"Of course. And I appreciate that."

It leads me to the next natural question. "Do you think I should tell him?"

I expected a strong reaction, but nowhere near the reaction I receive. "Are you serious? Absolutely not." Her eyes bulge as she stares at me. "No. Don't say a word about it."

"But—"

"Alexis. Not until you know for sure." For the first time in the better part of two decades, there's tenderness in her voice when she speaks of her ex-husband. Sorrow, too. "Honey, he's been through enough. Let's not heap this on him, not until you know for sure. I shudder to think what it would do to him even then."

Her voice trembles and reminds me that things weren't always bad for them. They used to be in love. So in love, it grossed us out when we were kids, me and Maddie both. "They're at it again!" she used to announce before pretending to gag. When you're a kid, you don't want to think of your parents as actual people. In your head, they only sprang into existence when you did. They didn't have lives of their own or dreams of their own before you came along. And they certainly didn't smooch in the kitchen or flirt openly.

What I wouldn't give to be grossed out just one more time. To look at my sister and roll my eyes and pretend to be sick because my parents love each other.

Mom runs a hand under her eyes again before releasing a shuttering sigh. "That was his choice, what he did," she whispers. "And he has suffered enough for it. We all have. I don't want to hurt him any worse until we're sure it's not all in vain. Do you understand what I'm saying?"

"I hear you. And I agree. I only wanted to get your opinion on it."

"Well, you have it now."

"I was thinking about going to the prison and speaking to him. Russell Duffy."

Her expression tightens like she's in pain. Like all it takes is hearing his name. "If you think it would help anything."

That's the thing. I'm not sure that it will help. I only know it feels like that's what I need to do next. To speak to him, to try to understand what happened. How he ended up as the scapegoat. What were the conditions of his arrest? Why did he seem like the natural suspect?

Maybe I just need to see him with my own eyes and hear his voice.

Though I doubt he'll want to see me.

15

"I see the years haven't slowed down your driving any."

Mitch's quiet comment makes me chuckle. It also makes me lessen the pressure on the gas pedal. "So arrest me. I'm in a hurry."

"When are you not in a hurry?"

"Oh, I don't know. There are definitely times when it makes sense to slow down. To relax, enjoy." I glance his way, arching an eyebrow.

His soft growl tells me he got the message. "Speaking of which, when can we engage in a little of that again?"

"Ooh, so romantic of you. Let's put a little one-on-one time on the calendar." I shiver and sigh before giggling.

I'm glad I invited him to come with me on this drive to Bangor. And not only because he makes me laugh hard enough that I can forget everything that's been weighing me down. His presence works magic on me. He makes everything more interesting, more fun, just by being around.

"I'll let you know," I finally offer.

"That doesn't sound very promising."

"Listen up, Mr. Dutton. You think I wouldn't much rather be at your place right now? Preferably under the covers?"

"I'm just teasing. Besides, this is business for me, too." I grin to myself at the excitement in his voice. He's picking up a new coffee roaster in Bangor, something he can use for the café. If anyone had told me back when we were in school that this would be the sort of thing he would be genuinely excited about one day, I would've laughed myself silly.

Now, I can understand why he's enthused about the purchase. I was thrilled when I bought my first Roomba. Amazing how time changes us.

"Check that out." Mitch points and I follow the direction to find a group of kids sledding on a hill, set far enough back from the road that there's no chance of ending up in traffic. My chest tightens at the sight. Naturally, I think of Cayden and his parents and their friends. I have to wonder if either of the other two couples present will ever let their kids out of their sight again. Not until they're grown, probably. I can't say I blame them. I would probably react the same way.

But that's not what Mitch is thinking of, because Mitch has the ability to see a bunch of kids involved in a perfectly natural, normal activity and not be plunged into darkness the way I am. "Remember when we used to sled? Back on the hill behind the high school?"

"Oh, you mean the hill where you broke your collarbone?"

"Listen, I'm not the one who told Jimmy Schaeffer to stand right in my path. There I am, yelling at him to get out of the way, and he's just standing there gaping at me, watching me rush at him. The idiot."

"And you were the one who ended up hurt."

"That's the way it always is, right?"

"More often than not," I agree. "I wonder what he's up to nowadays."

"Married, four kids, runs a body shop outside of town. I take my car in to see him when I'm having trouble."

He laughs. "And he always gives me a discount. He says it's because we're old buddies, but I can't lie.

The first time I took it in, I sort of made it a point to rub my collarbone like it was aching."

"You didn't!" I squeal.

"Well, it sort of does in bad weather, and it was raining at the time…" He trails off with a shrug while I laugh harder than I have in ages.

"Hey, you've gotta do what you gotta do."

It's funny. When we have conversations like that one, I feel so young again. Not that I'm exactly old, even though when I was in high school, the idea of turning thirty was enough to frighten me. Thirty was ancient. Thirty meant the best part of your life was already over. But what did I know?

Besides. What was the alternative? Dying young? There has already been enough of that in my family.

Even though we're out together because I'm researching something for a case, I feel happier by the time I drop him off so he can pick up his fancy roaster. I'm more myself than I've been in days. He fills me up. He makes me remember who I am. It's so easy to forget. I have a bad habit of losing myself in cases, putting my needs aside in favor of working. Mitch brings me back to center. He reminds me of what matters.

"I won't be long," I promise before he closes the door and mercifully spares me the cold air leaking into the car. I only thought I remembered how bitter late fall could be around here. Vague memory is nothing when compared to the real thing.

I continue to the security company whose headquarters is only ten minutes away. The building sits in an office park, with gray, nondescript buildings lined up in rows. It's sort of bleak, really, especially with the trees stripped bare and so much snow piled up wherever the plows dumped it. Snow that's starting to get gray and dirty. What a shame it doesn't stay pristine forever, but then that's true of so many things in life.

I follow the signs pointing me to the building in question, then park beside a van boasting the company logo on the side. New England Security. Short, to the point. What a shame they don't advertise their penchant for hidden cameras.

As soon as I step through the swinging door and into a rather soulless lobby, I head straight for the reception desk set up against the wall beneath the company logo. The stainless steel letters gleam beneath fluorescent lights. "What can I help you with today?" a middle-aged receptionist asks, wearing a pleasant smile. Something tells me she won't feel so pleasant once she gets wind of why I'm here.

"Is there a manager I can speak to?"

Her mouth opens, then snaps shut when I show her my badge. "I'm here to inquire about work that was done on a property in Broken Hill. Who can I speak to about that?"

"I'm not sure." Her fingers fly over a keyboard and her eyes dart over the screen. I can't see what she's doing. I hope she's not giving someone the heads up, warning them of my presence.

"As I said," I remind her in a light but firm voice, "I want to speak to someone in management. The higher up, the better."

"Exactly what is this about?"

"That's something I would like to discuss with whomever it is you point me toward. But it does have to do with an active investigation," I add, in case that will light a fire under her.

"I see." She picks up the phone and presses one of the buttons on the switchboard. "Frank? There's an FBI agent out here who wants to speak to you." I have to wonder what Frank is thinking right now. I wish she hadn't come out and announced I was with the FBI, but that might be what gets him out here quickly. It might also give him time to destroy evidence.

As it turns out, there's no chance of him doing that, since the man she called is sitting in a glass walled office behind me. She looks over my shoulder and I turn to find him setting down the receiver and standing, straightening his tie before opening his door and taking long strides across the lobby.

"Frank Miller." The rather short, pudgy man engulfs my hand in a tight grip before backing away. "What can I do for you, Miss…"

"Agent Forrest." I flash my badge before adding, "I work out of our Boston field office, but at the present moment, I'm working along with the Broken Hill Police Department. I have a few questions about the work done at a property in the area. I understand your company installed cameras."

"We do a lot of that." He chuckles affably, then gestures toward his office. "Why don't you step inside and we can have a conversation? Can I get you anything to drink?" I turn him down, noting how warm and cordial he's behaving. I can't tell yet whether that's an act or not.

"Now." Once I've taken a seat across from him, he sinks into his chair while I pull out a notepad. "Which property are you concerned with? We do manage security for so many."

"This is a series of cabins up by Lake Morgan."

He pauses in the middle of typing on his laptop. "Oh. We don't manage that property any longer."

"I understand, but I also understand it was your company that first handled the installation. Is that correct?"

"It is." His steely eyes harden. He's not playing Mr. Nice Guy anymore. "Exactly what brings you here? Is there some trouble with the work we did down there?"

"I'm not entirely sure as of yet, which is why I'm here. So you installed cameras around the property?"

"That's right."

"About how long ago was that?"

He returns to his laptop, and I notice his fingers strike the keys a little harder than they did before. "That was nine months ago, when our company was first hired. Until then, there were no cameras on the property."

"Do you still have access to the feeds?"

This time, there's no hesitation. "Absolutely not. We install the equipment and service it as necessary, but the feeds are handled by the management companies. That's always been our policy."

"Is it your policy to keep a record of the employees who were involved in a specific installation?"

"Certainly. We keep records of all of that."

"Then maybe you can tell me who installed cameras inside the cabins along with those throughout the property."

"That's impossible." He even barks out a laugh.

"And why is that?"

"Because we didn't install cameras on the interiors. Only the exterior. It's right here in my system."

"Then I'm going to need the name of the technician who handled that installation." I pull up a photo I took of the camera in the bathroom of the Duncan cabin. "I took that picture two days ago. That was one of three cameras I found in one cabin, and I found a similar set up in the next cabin over. I didn't have time to inspect all of them, but that told me all I needed to know."

"This isn't right." He shakes his head, scowling. "This is not our policy."

"Then I'm going to need the name of the person who installed it. Because the people staying there certainly had no idea they were being recorded while showering and sleeping and everything else."

"That's just terrible." He types something, then pulls out a small notepad and jots down information. "His name is Julian Oates. Young guy, late twenties, lives not far from here. According to his file, he's no longer with the company."

Convenient. "I would like to speak to him."

"By all means." He tears off a slip of paper and hands it to me. "Here's his last known address and phone number. Please, we would be glad to work with you on this. We have nothing to hide here."

As I leave, I ask myself whether the sweat on his upper lip was from fear, or simply a natural reaction after being questioned by an FBI agent. I guess you don't have to be a bad guy to get a little nervous in a situation like that.

I wonder how Julian Oates will react.

16

"Let me get this straight. You want me to come with you to question a guy?"

The excitement in Mitch's voice is much too adorable. "Pump the brakes."

"I'm just saying. Is that what you're suggesting? You want me to be part of the investigation?"

"This is not supposed to be a fun little outing," I remind him. "And it doesn't mean you're part of the investigation. You happen to be with me while I question a person of interest."

"Well, that's not very exciting."

I shouldn't laugh and encourage him, but it's not easy being serious when he is determined to lighten my spirits. "I'm just saying, you happen to be here with me. I don't see the point in driving all the way back to Broken Hill, then all the way out here again."

"Of course, it wouldn't make any sense."

"Which means you will be with me while I track this guy down."

"And if things get tricky, I can help."

"No. That is exactly what you will not be doing."

"What if you need help?"

"I don't like to throw this around," I murmur while following the directions on my GPS, "but I am sort of a trained FBI agent. I can handle some guy who used to work for a security company. We're not talking about some criminal kingpin here, you know?"

"Who's to say we're not?"

"I would prefer you hang back. It would make me feel a lot better if I knew you were safe and sound."

"Funny. I'm usually the one telling you to be safe and stop taking so many chances."

"And you know how it feels when I don't listen," I retort before sticking out my tongue. "So don't do it to me. Got it?"

"Fine, fine," he grumbles good-naturedly. "Do you think this guy installed the cameras in the cabins?"

It doesn't take much reflection to come up with an answer. "I do. That Frank guy back at the security company didn't have the first idea what I was talking about, and he turned as white as a sheet."

"I imagine he knows darn well what will happen if it gets out that his company is allowing something like this to slip through the cracks."

"He was certainly surprised. And a little sweaty."

"Guess I would be, too."

The closer we get to the address Frank provided, the more uneasy I become. Maybe it's not a bad idea to have Mitch here with me. As much as I detest the idea of using a man to feel more secure, facts are facts. Statistically, an attacker is less likely to approach a woman when she's in the presence of a man. Alone? That's another story. But a man might fight back.

I doubt anyone could tell at first glance that they're dealing with an FBI agent. I have no doubt I could handle myself. I would rather not be put in that position, is all. I've had enough close calls as of late.

"I'm already starting to get an idea of who this guy is." Mitch catches himself and gives me a guilty look while we wait for a red light to change. "Sounds pretty low, doesn't it?"

"I understand what you're saying. It isn't like I wasn't thinking the same thing," I murmur while watching a woman dressed in layers of filthy clothing push a shopping cart full of trash bags through the crosswalk. While I never want to get caught up in ugly stereotypes, this neighborhood is unpleasant—putting it mildly. Its sidewalks are littered with garbage, broken glass, crumpled up papers and cigarette butts. Weeds grow through too many cracks to be counted. The buildings themselves are falling apart, some with boarded windows, others with front porches that sag dangerously. A few of the buildings don't have front doors. And it's so very cold.

I can't hide my relief when I turn the corner and drive a few blocks down to find a dilapidated, but less dangerous looking building with Julian Oates's address written in black sharpie on the front of the mailbox. "I'm going to go up and talk to him."

"You're going to go up there alone?"

"That was the idea, yes."

Mitch holds an arm out across my chest the way he would if he wanted to protect me from a crash. As if that would stop me from getting out of the car. "I don't feel comfortable with this. I really don't. All joking aside."

"I can appreciate that, but this is something I have to do alone. I can't involve you."

I pull to a stop in front of a two-story building covered in siding that may at one time have been white. Now it's a dirty gray, with the paint chipped off in a million places. Beside the building is an empty lot surrounded by a chain-link fence. The abundant weeds, old tires and garbage bags visible from where I parked tell a story.

It's the staircase running alongside the building that holds my attention. According to the information I received, Julian lives on the second floor, and I would imagine that's the means of accessing his apartment. "You're going to walk up that?" Mitch shoves his hands into his back pockets upon stepping out of the car. "I don't like this. It looks like those stairs are ready to collapse at any second."

"Well, it's only as far as the second floor," I reason. "If I fall, the worst I'll do is break something." His distraught expression makes me regret my joke. "Sorry. I'll be fine. I'm not going to fall."

"Sure, you say that now."

The fact is, I'm not much looking forward to climbing the stairs, but it's the only way of coming face-to-face with this guy. I'm certainly not going to let him go just because I was spooked by his living conditions. No investigation would ever go anywhere if something so trivial brought everything to a halt. "I'm just going to go up there and see if he's home. I'll be fine."

"Just the same, I hope you don't mind if I wait around out here."

"Be my guest." It's cute how concerned he is. I would never say that out loud to him, though. I wouldn't want to embarrass him.

The sky is a foreboding shade of gray, but that could be my imagination getting the best of me as I start up the steps. They creak and groan alarmingly, but I do my best to ignore it, taking one step after another, my heart pounding a little harder the higher I climb. I doubt he would be much of a threat, but who's to say? I could be dealing with a career criminal for all I know, even if a quick Google search on Julian's name didn't bring up any arrest warrants or mugshots. He could be flying under the radar. After all, if there's anything I've learned lately, it's how easy it is to overlook an evil monster even when they're hiding in plain sight.

I can't think about that now. One problem at a time.

I have to pretend not to notice the way the entire staircase sways ever so slightly once I reach the landing at the top. It makes me wonder how securely the stairs are attached to the wall. Of all things I really don't need to think about right now, that's up there at the top of the list. The sooner I get this over with, the better.

But when I knock, there's no answer. I try again, then lean close to the door, closing my eyes to focus. It doesn't seem like there's any sound coming from inside, either. No TV, no conversation. I'm sure if I asked Mitch to wait around with me, he would do so without complaining.

Glass crunches down on the sidewalk and I turn, prepared to tell Mitch to get back in the car. Only it isn't Mitch at the foot of the stairs. It's a tall, lanky young man with shoulder-length, dirty blonde hair he wears in a mullet. When did they come back in style? Despite the bitter cold, he only wears an unzipped hoodie over an old Metallica T-shirt and a pair of baggy jeans. He's carrying a bottle of soda in one hand, a lit cigarette in the other.

And when he notices me standing in front of his door, he pauses, coming to stop at the foot of the stairs. "Can I help you?" he asks in a deep voice.

"Maybe. Are you Julian Oates?"

"If I am?" Rather than wait, he begins climbing, and his smirk widens into a smile that becomes more pronounced with every step.

"Then you're just the man I want to see."

"I hear that a lot." Something tells me that is not true, but I'll smile anyway. "And who are you?"

"My name is Alexis Forrest."

"And why are you here, Alexis Forrest?" It takes all of my self-control not to shudder in revulsion at his overly familiar tone. Now that he's closer to me, I can see the pitiful attempt at a mustache growing above his upper lip—and the cold sore he's trying and failing to conceal.

My badge catches the light filtering through the clouds. "I'm an FBI agent, and I have a few questions."

He comes to a stop two steps down from where I'm waiting. The cigarette falls from his fingers. His already pale complexion goes white.

And he turns to run.

"Stop!" I'm talking to myself. He takes a few steps before deciding that's not fast enough, and then vaults over the railing and lands on the ground between the stairs and the fence. Somehow, he manages to do it without slowing himself down, while all I can do is run down the stairs at top speed. But he's already too far ahead of me, rounding the building at a full run.

"Mitch!" I shout once I reach the ground and sprint around the building.

I only intended to warn him of what was coming. I wasn't asking for backup.

But Mitch has ideas of his own. Just now, his idea was to knock Julian Oates face-first onto the sidewalk, where he waits with a knee pressed against the kid's back to hold him in place.

I come to a stop, breathing harder than I like, while Mitch raises an eyebrow. "What was that about not needing help?" He is lucky he looks so incredibly hot right now, or I might have a few sharp words for him.

"Very funny."

"What is this?" Julian demands. "Get off me! I can't breathe!"

I go down on one knee in front of Julian, whose ghostly complexion has now gone dark red. "Nice try, but people who can't breathe can't shout, Julian. What happened back there? You seemed so interested in me until I showed you my badge."

"I didn't do anything!"

"Just the same, I would like to have a conversation with you down at the local police station." I make the call from my cell while Mitch holds Julian in place. He must have decided it's no use fighting, since he lies still, muttering an occasional profanity under his breath.

17

"Thank you so much for your cooperation."

Captain Brenner waves me off, wearing an affable grin. "It isn't every day I get a chance to work with other departments. And I know your Captain Felch down there in Broken Hill. He's never hesitated to offer assistance when we needed it."

That sounds like him. "How's our subject?"

"About how you would expect after cooling his jets for a couple of hours in an interrogation room. We informed him about the warrant to search his place." He shakes his head, wearing a smirk. "Needless to say, he didn't take it well."

I wouldn't take it well if I had the sort of secrets he does. "Can't say I feel sorry for him."

"Nor do I." He exhales and rolls his shoulders back. "Would you like to lead off?"

The memory of Krista Duncan's horror is fresh, potent. "Nothing would please me more."

As soon as we enter the room, Justin sits up straighter. "When can I leave? I've got work to do. I'm gonna lose my job over this."

"Justin. I think we both know you don't have a job. That's not how you make your money." I take a seat across from him and sigh. "You know there was a search warrant. You have to know your laptop was taken away to be used as evidence. And already, it's told us a lot."

Amazing. Even now, he looks like he doesn't believe me. He probably doesn't want to. I suppose I can't blame him, though I certainly feel no pity.

"Now. Let's talk seriously. We both know what they found in your files. It would be in your best interest to cooperate fully with me and with the Bangor PD."

"I need a cigarette," he blurts out.

"I can have your pack brought in. It was still in your pocket when you got here." The captain gets up and opens the door, murmuring something to whoever's on the other side while I maintain my steady stare at the man in front of me. He goes out of his way to avoid my gaze like the coward he is. "Now. Julian. I have it on record from your previous employer that you installed the security cameras at the property on Morgan Lake, down in Broken Hill."

"Yeah, that's right." He squirms in the chair, tapping his fingers against the table in a rapid beat that brings to mind machine gun fire.

"And can you tell me where you installed cameras?"

"Like, specifically?" He has the nerve to scoff. "No. It was months ago."

"I was thinking generally. Can you remember the general locations where cameras were installed?"

"I don't know. Outside, so the management company could keep an eye on stuff? That's pretty much the reason anybody wants those cameras installed. I barely remember doing it."

Lies. Even now, he's lying to me. He has to know it's useless. Or maybe he doesn't. Maybe he thinks I'm bluffing. He is entirely wrong.

"Come on, now," I murmur, shaking my head. "We both know there's more to it than that."

"Don't tell me what I know," he warns with a growl that only hardens my determination to see him behind bars.

"Don't lie to me," I counter, still wearing a smile I don't feel. "You're lying to me now when you say you only installed cameras on the exterior of the property. I know that's not true."

"How do you know that?"

"Because we have your laptop, remember?" I fold my arms on the scarred table and lean in a little, like I'm sharing a secret. "See, there are people trained specifically to hack into computers. It's all legal, of course. That's what the warrant is for. A judge signed off on it and gave the cops permission to take your laptop as evidence and go through everything you've saved on it."

I lower my brow as well as my voice. "Now. I am going to give you one last chance to come clean and acknowledge what existed in those files before this gets serious. I'm trying to give you a break here. Work with me, and this doesn't have to be as bad as it would be if you resisted."

He's sweating, moistening his lips with the tip of his tongue, while his gaze darts around furtively. When the door opens and an officer comes in holding a half-crushed pack of cigarettes, he reaches forward with a trembling hand and takes a few moments to light up.

I exchange a look with the captain, and I see how concerned he is. I know why. Julian was read his rights, but he has not yet mentioned a lawyer. It's his right to have one present while answering questions, but we don't have to provide one until he asks.

In other words, it would be in his best interest not to say a word until a lawyer arrives. But aside from reading him his rights, we are not obligated to provide one. So he can spill his guts here and now without the benefit of legal counsel, which is nothing but good news for us.

"Okay." He takes a drag from his cigarette and blows the cloud of smoke toward the ceiling. "So I added cameras inside the cabins, too."

"What was the purpose of the installation?"

"There's people who pay good money for that kind of footage."

A hand closes around my stomach and squeezes tight. "Did you provide them with that footage?"

His head bobs up and down. "Yeah. There's a lot of sickos out there. They wanna see all kinds of things." As if that releases him from any guilt. As far as he's concerned, he's providing a service. Am I supposed to relate to him?

"And where are they paying this good money?"

"Encrypted servers. Dark web stuff. I never get any names. I want you to know that. Nobody ever uses their real name, so I can't help you track them down.

I believe that. Who would want to leave themselves open to prosecution? The people involved in this sort of activity don't take chances. "What did you receive in exchange?"

He scoffs before taking another drag. The stench is nauseating I know I'll have it in my hair after this. "Man, you already know."

"Once again. Cooperate, and this will go better than it could otherwise. Dig in your heels, refuse to tell me what I need to know, and there's only so much I can do to help."

He doesn't believe me, that much is clear. But he doesn't have any other choice, either. He's savvy enough to understand that. "Crypto. They paid in cryptocurrency."

"Did they pay well?"

"They do—they did."

"What happened?"

His head falls back and stares at the ceiling while his cigarette burns between his fingers. "It was a scam. The owner of the wallet embezzled all the funds. They're gone. I lost everything."

Poor baby. I don't pretend to know a lot about cryptocurrency, but from what I've already learned from the captain before coming in to speak with Julian, the story checks out. And that's exactly why

I can't bring myself to take crypto seriously. It's too easy to lose your shirt to some stranger halfway around the world.

"Then I guess it was all for nothing," I murmur while he cringes and rubs a fist over his eyes, then takes another drag of his cigarette.

"Yeah. I guess so."

"When was the last time you sold footage?"

"People are buying it all the time. It's not like we do an introduction before there's a transaction. Somebody could be buying it right now. I really don't know."

"And is there any way to know how many times a certain piece of footage was purchased to download?"

He snickers before folding his arms. "You're all the big experts. You have the laptop. You tell me."

So much for cooperation. I stand and give him one final stare before turning away and leaving the room. The captain follows me and grumbles under his breath once the door is closed. "How does a person live without a conscience?"

"I think that's exactly what it is, too," I admit. "Either you're born without one, or you have to fight so hard to survive, you realize you can't afford one. But this guy had a decent job. And obviously, he installed those cameras while he was still employed. He has no excuse."

"Well, if you're satisfied, we'll take it from here."

But I'm not satisfied. That's the thing. Sure, he won't be able to violate strangers anymore, but the footage has already been downloaded and viewed countless times. And if someone can download it, they can share it. It would be like tearing up a feather pillow on a windy day, then trying to collect the feathers after they've blown away. Impossible, in other words.

That's why when I meet up with Mitch near the front door of the station, I'm not smiling. "I thought you'd be happy you caught him," he says as we leave, both of us immediately buttoning our coats once we get a feel of the icy air. There was plenty of time to get warm in the station while we waited for word from the judge. Mitch waited all that time… not that he had a choice considering I drove, but no matter how many times I offered to take him home or pay for an Uber, he insisted on staying.

"Sure, but it feels pointless. The damage has been done, and I'm not any closer to finding out who took Cayden." And shot at me, but he does not need to be reminded of that. Frankly, I would like not having to think about it, myself.

"You can't save the whole world." He wraps an arm around me and pulls me close as we walk to the car. "You can only do what you can do."

"No offense, but that sounds like something from a fortune cookie."

At least he chuckles at my half-hearted joke. "Now that you mention it, I could go for Chinese. I think after helping you catch a criminal, the least you can do is buy me dinner."

"You drive a hard bargain."

He opens the door for me even though I'm the one driving, then pulls me in by my hips. "Yeah, but I'm worth it."

"Listen to you. You are certainly feeling good about yourself, now that you've collared your first criminal."

His baby blues twinkle in the most enticing way. "Maybe later, I can show you just how good I'm feeling."

Even if I didn't desperately need a diversion, there would be no way of resisting him. "I'm going to hold you to that."

18

"What's that? An apple for the teacher?"

All I can do is throw a glance Andy's way as I walk through the station carrying a cardboard cup holder from Mitch's shop. "Jealous?" I ask with a sweet smile. At least he seems like a decent sport about it, chuckling and shaking his head. The more time I spend here, the easier it is to understand him and to deal with him. I can't take his heckling personally. It's safer to think of him as a pesky older brother figure. We don't have to be adversaries. And I know from experience he's a decent cop—at least when he's focused on work and not on making jokes.

I don't have any need to kiss up to the captain, but he is the man I need to see first thing this morning, and he's always tired. Besides, I was raised to believe

KATE GABLE

it's rude to show up somewhere with refreshments and not include some for others.

"You're too thoughtful." Captain Felch turns away from his computer screen when I set the carrier on his desk. It means pushing aside a handful of papers it's been a while since he's straightened up around here.

"I figured you could use something a little stronger and tastier than what comes out of that machine in the break room or the truck outside."

"I've been spoiled by espresso," he admits with a sheepish grin. "Still, you don't need to spend the money."

"Don't worry about that. I got them for free."

"I suppose I can accept, then." He eyes me, appraising. "Exactly how did you manage that? Nothing illegal, I hope?"

"It's nice to have friends in high places."

"Well, thank you." He pops the spout on the plastic lid and takes a deep inhale before sipping. "Oh, that is nice. Drip coffee has nothing on a nice cappuccino."

"In case you're ever curious, I now know more about coffee roasters than I ever thought possible. I'd be happy to educate you if you're interested."

"So you had an interesting trip to Bangor. What can you tell me about Julian Oates?"

"I can report he makes my skin crawl. But something tells me that's not what you were asking."

"Not precisely, but thank you for the insight."

"He made a pretty penny, selling footage from those cameras. He installed them in several locations, not only Lake Morgan. There's roughly a year's worth of footage out there, circulating all over the dark web."

"Horrible."

I shudder at the thought of knowing there's footage of me out there somewhere, knowing others have watched it. Having no idea how far the videos have spread. There's no such thing as putting the toothpaste back in the tube. It would be impossible to scrub the footage from the internet at this point.

"The implications are nauseating." The captain sips his coffee again and lets out a soft murmur of appreciation, but I'm sure it would make Mitch happy if he heard it.

"Sure. Kids, adults. Bedroom activities, showers. It's the ultimate violation."

"And I'm guessing your guy didn't offer any remorse over what he's done."

"No, but he was very sorry he got caught. And that all of his ill-gotten gains were stolen."

"Imagine. Selling your soul for nothing."

"Pretty much." Although I highly doubt this was Justin's first offense. You don't just wake up one morning and decide you're going to sell hidden camera footage online. For all we know, he could have chosen that job deliberately, knowing how easily he could use it to make extra on the side.

"What do we think about him being Cayden's killer?"

"He has an alibi."

"Verifiable?"

I can't help but grin at the irony. "He was running errands all day. The laundromat, the grocery store, and he stopped in at the local bar later in the afternoon to pick up a couple of six packs to get him through the blizzard. Security footage confirms it."

His wry grin tells me he gets the not-very-funny joke. To think, it was a security camera that bailed him out, at least when it comes to Cayden's kidnapping and murder.

"Anyway," I continue as I take a seat, "he doesn't match the physical description of the guy I saw out there."

"I wasn't aware you caught such a good look at him with all that snow everywhere."

"I didn't exactly get a clear look at his face, but I did see his shape. He was taller, much bulkier. Julian is too lanky." I'm sure he hears the frustration in my voice. I'm not exactly trying to hide it, after all. I realize it would be too much to ask, finding the killer so easily. But I could use a win. I need one.

"What are the odds the man who took Cayden was one of Julian's ... customers?" His lip curls in disgust.

"I thought about that." I've done more than think about it. I spent most of the drive home last night talking it out with Mitch. As always, he was a wonderful listener, a sounding board, not to mention a leveling presence. He kept me calm, kept me from letting my imagination run away with me. Somehow, he understands me and even appreciates how hard I find it to separate my work from my personal life.

"Any conclusions?"

"There's a definite chance. Somebody spends a day watching a family in a cabin. Observing. They're eating dinner together, watching TV, spending quality time. For some people, it's not enough just to watch."

"What does a person get out of that? I'm not talking about footage from the bathroom or the bedroom."

We share a knowing look that speaks volumes without him having to elaborate. "But footage from the kitchen?"

"There are all sorts of reasons voyeurism takes root. It all depends on the person. Sometimes, it's the thrill of watching someone and knowing they have no idea. It's a sense of power. A deity watching from on high. For others, it's a means of experiencing what they didn't in their past, either when they were children or as they got older. A happy family life. They can be quite powerful, especially if the voyeur tells himself he's part of things. A fantasy that has nothing to do with sexual fulfillment. It's more like wish fulfillment."

Then I shrug helplessly. "And sometimes, it's a case of a kink gone too far. Eventually, watching videos that were set up to create the illusion of power aren't enough. The way a drug user develops a tolerance over time. It's the same with this. The brain isn't getting the dopamine it's used to, so the voyeur needs to up the ante. Footage like this, there's no question of whether the subject is really unaware they're being watched. There's nothing staged, the way it might be on an adult site or something like that."

"Just when you think you've seen the worst of what humanity is capable of…"

"In situations like this, the perpetrator may also have difficulty relating to others. Remembering other people are just that, other people. Individuals like themselves. There's usually a history of separation. And inability to form meaningful connections with others, because whether consciously or otherwise, the perpetrator only considers himself or herself real. And besides, if the victim never finds out, nobody got hurt."

"Oh, I'm well aware of the amount of rationalization that can go on in the mind of certain types of criminals." He finishes off his coffee and tosses the cup into his wastebasket with a sigh. "So the theory we're working on is, one of Julian's customers decided it wasn't enough to watch from afar anymore. He had to get to know his subject personally."

"It does seem logical in a twisted way." Which is why it gives me no joy to shrug. "Then again, there's a chance it was merely a crime of opportunity. Of Cayden being in the wrong place at the wrong time. This guy could've been driving down the road, minding his business, when he happened upon a little boy sledding by himself. A small boy, one who wouldn't fight too hard." I close my eyes, shaking my head. "I can't forget the footage I watched. There he was, having the time of his life with his new sled. I wanted to …"

"You wanted to stop him. I've been there. It's not easy."

"He was so small." I close my eyes, but it's not enough. I can still almost feel him in my arms, his limp little body that weighed practically nothing. Sure, it hadn't seemed that way when I was trudging through so much snow, but I might not have ever made it back to the car if he were much bigger. He didn't stand a chance, which is exactly the sort of thing a predator looks for in their victim.

"And what does the therapist think about this?"

My eyes open to find him wearing a knowing smirk. "Message received," I mumble.

"I don't think you have received it. Alexis, you need to speak to someone. Maybe you can't see what this has done to you, but I can. Why do you insist on punishing yourself?"

"I'm not trying to do any such thing. But there are only so many hours in the day, you know? I'm running down leads day and night."

"You find the time, and that's an order. Unless you want me to take this to your superiors."

The man wants to play hardball, does he? "I get it." Though I might not bring him coffee for a while, just the same. It makes him a little too aggressive and prone to speaking to me like he's my father.

"Good."

"In the meantime, I'm going to dig into Julian's customer list. There has to be a way to find information on the people who made those transactions. There might be some who live close enough to the area to make them a person of interest."

"That sounds like a plan. But I mean what I said. You have to take care of yourself. Otherwise, you won't be any good to Cayden's family."

I wasn't any good to them initially. I need to shake off the guilt. It's one of the reasons the captain wants me to see the therapist in the first place. I can't let it go. I should have found him sooner, somehow. Even if I'm being completely unfair to myself, and totally unrealistic, there's still that part of me that feels like I failed. Because I, of all people, know what happens to a family in the wake of a tragedy like this. In the case of the Duncans, they don't have another child to love, someone to keep them moving forward.

And even though things went so terribly wrong for my family, I know my parents tried their best to keep it together for my sake. It just wasn't enough. Their grief was too powerful, too heavy, and it pulled them so far down into darkness, they lost sight of me.

I wanted so much to spare that nice couple the same pain.

Since that's not possible, I decide to do the next best thing by heading to my temporary office and beginning a dive into the individuals who have been identified so far. Unfortunately, the call I placed to Bangor PD gets me nowhere. "The forensics team is still digging through the records. All the information is encrypted, but we are working with the Bureau in hopes of getting somewhere quickly."

"Please, let me know as soon as you find anything so I can start asking questions." I'm sure it won't take much time, especially with the Bureau involved, but I wanted to start digging in now. Today. It was challenging enough, having to sit on my hands and wait last night. Granted, Mitch made it a lot easier. He is just about the nicest distraction I can think of, and I went out of my way to focus solely on him once we got back in from Bangor and feasted on General Tso's chicken and pork lo mein. It's easy to lose sight of what matters when I'm overcome by a case for one reason or another, but that's exactly when I need to pay the most attention to the good things in my life. And he most certainly qualifies. I'm starting to wonder how I ever got through without him, which might be dangerous. Letting myself get too attached again, when nothing about this assignment in Broken Hill was meant to be permanent.

But I already made the mistake of shutting him out of my life once before. I'm not sure I could bring myself to do it again. It's enough to make my head hurt, so I push the thoughts aside in favor of shooting him a text. How about dinner again tonight? I could use the company.

And the thing is, I can set the phone aside with confidence, knowing he'll say yes.

19

It's closing in on six o'clock and my eyes burn from all of the reading and research I've done today. There's a lot I don't know about certain things that pertain to the case. Like crypto. Goodness knows I've heard enough about it, but I've never really understood it. After part of the afternoon spent learning about it, I can't say I'm much more of an expert. One thing I've picked up on, though, it's the preferred method of completing transactions like the ones that went on between Julian and the viewers who purchased his videos. No pesky bank records getting in the way. It's also very volatile and risky, as Julian learned.

Captain Felch wondered if it was worth it, selling one's soul for nothing. I have to wonder if Julian had one to sell in the first place. How broken do you have to be to prey upon people that way?

Mitch and I aren't supposed to meet up until seven. Though it means driving out of my way, I decide to head out to Mom's house and grab a shower and a change of clothes. I'll be killing two birds with one stone, too, since I know she'll be thrilled to pieces when I announce I'm going to Mitch's. Not exactly the sort of mother-daughter talk I feel like having, but considering we went three years with barely any contact at all, I guess there's a lot of discomfort to catch up on.

Before closing out my Outlook program, I find an email that came through within the last few minutes. My pulse picks up speed when I note the sender: the Maine Department of Corrections.

Agent Forrest

Our records reflect your request for a visit with inmate Russell Duffy. Currently, there is a seven-week waitlist for such visitation; however, due to a last-minute cancellation, an opening has become available tomorrow. Your professional credentials along with your personal connection to the inmate in question leads us to extend this visitation to you if your schedule permits. Please contact our office at your earliest convenience to confirm your ability to appear for an interview tomorrow.

Tomorrow. There I was, figuring it would take forever to get approval to see him. Now I'm looking at the very real possibility of seeing him tomorrow.

My hand hovers over the desk phone, but I hesitate before drawing my head back. I should call. I should confirm.

Do I want to?

"I FEEL TERRIBLE."

"Physically? Are you sick? You're probably nervous, is all." Mitch offers a sympathetic look from the other side of the table. We decided to make up for the date we didn't get to have the night of the blizzard. Now, we're seated in the same booth we sat in the night I accidentally ran into him at The Tipsy Traveler.

"I was thinking more along the lines of guilt, since all we've done so far is talk about me."

"It just so happens you're one of my favorite subjects."

"Do you ever get tired of being so stinking charming?"

"What can I say? It's who I am. I can't help it." His blue eyes twinkle as he takes a long gulp of his pumpkin beer.

"Have I told you lately how grateful I am for you?"

He pretends to think about it, squinting and stroking his chin. "Not recently. But you did seem pretty grateful to me for stopping that sicko before he could run away from you yesterday."

"You are going to hold that over my head until the end of time, aren't you?"

"Only until there's something new to tease you about."

"Well, I am grateful. I don't want you to ever think I'm not. I don't know how I would get through life right now if it weren't for you, and I mean that. Just in case you ever feel like I don't appreciate you. It's important that you know I do."

He finally goes serious, nudging my leg under the table. "Hey. Certain things, you don't need to say. Not you. Not to me. I know you too well."

"If you know me so well, then tell me what to do. Should I go tomorrow?"

"His brows draw together and the smile slides off his face. "It depends."

"On what?"

"For one thing, on what you hope to learn. I was unaware you even put in for a visit."

That would be because I didn't tell anybody. "It was a spur of the moment thing. After we found the cabin."

"Right. Are you sure you're up to that?"

"That's the thing. I won't know until I get there, will I?"

"Have you ever been in the same room with that man?"

"No, never. I was too young to sit through the trial."

"Of course. And what do you plan on asking him about, if there was any plan in mind?"

This is wonderful dinner conversation—but I doubt he'd let me drop the subject now. He's too interested in what I have to say. "I'm dying to know the circumstances behind his arrest. I need to know why they made him the scapegoat, if he was the scapegoat at all. I need to know …"

My throat closes and I looked down at the table, blinking back sudden tears. "I need to know if the wrong man has been suffering for this all these years."

"And what do you think you would gain from that?" His question is gentle. He's not pushing, he's not accusing, there isn't even any sort of opinion half-hidden in his tone of voice or his choice of words. He's genuinely asking.

"I'm not sure," I have to admit. "At the time, it seemed important that I see him. Now that the possibility is right here in front of me, I can't quite remember why it seems so important."

"Well, I don't think anything would necessarily be lost by you going out there, other than some more gas and mileage on your car." When all I do is snicker, he reaches across the table and takes my chin in his hand, lifting my head. "I know you. You'll curse yourself until you're blue in the face if you don't take advantage of this opportunity."

"You're not wrong," I admit.

"And if you need a little support, I'm happy to make the drive with you."

"You don't have to do that."

"Who said anything about have to? Maybe I was looking for an excuse to take another road trip. Voila, an opportunity fell into my lap."

"Don't you have a business to run?"

"What's the point of having employees if you can't let them handle things sometimes?"

And that's how, the following morning, I end up on the road with Mitch for the second time in three days. This time, I am considerably more anxious. "Maybe I should cancel," I fret before we're more than fifteen miles outside of town.

Mitch reaches for his coffee cup, nestled beside mine in the console cup holder. "If you think that is for the best, I wouldn't stop you."

"You sound like my mother."

"What? You didn't tell her you're doing this, did you?"

"No! That's not what I meant," I assure him before barking out a laugh. "I mean, you have a way of choosing your words carefully. If that's what you think is best, dear," I say, in a singsong, know-it-all sort of voice.

"Is that how I sound?" he mutters.

"Pretty close." I glance his way to find him chuckling. "You must have an actual opinion. You can't be neutral all the time."

"What difference does my opinion make?"

"It makes a lot of difference, and don't act like you don't know it."

"Maybe I just wanted to hear you say it." He nudges my leg playfully until I can't help but laugh.

"Sometimes you are too cute for your own good."

"Honestly? I think you should go through with it. I know you're strong enough to handle whatever happens, and I know for sure you'll beat yourself up if you chicken out."

"I'm not sure I would call it chickening out, but I get your point." I can't shake the nervous energy twisting me up no matter how much sense it makes for me to take advantage of this chance. "What if he's awful? What if he curses me out or brags about killing Maddie?"

"Even if he doesn't?"

"Remember, I don't know for sure whether or not he did. But I mean, he spent all these years in prison. Either he's innocent, and he hates my family for helping put him in prison, or he's guilty and he still hates my family."

"Or he doesn't hate anybody. You won't know until you get there. Don't prepare for trouble you haven't encountered yet, and maybe never will."

"I know you're right."

"But …"

"But, there are still so many questions. So many doubts."

"Listen. You absolutely don't have to do this. You realize that, right? Nobody is forcing you. If it doesn't feel right, we can turn around right now, and you'll have lost nothing."

He's right about that, too. He's worried about so many things. It's almost unfair, frankly. I wonder what it's like, being so calm and level headed.

A few more miles pass on the odometer before I make up my mind. Not that there's much of a decision to be made. Not that there was much chance of me turning around and walking away at this point. "No. I'm going. Like you said, I'd kick myself in the pants until I couldn't sit without wincing if I passed up on this."

"Exactly what I thought." He sounds pretty pleased with himself as he continues drinking his coffee while the sun breaches the eastern horizon.

20

"This is insane."

Mitch turns away from where he's been gazing out toward the imposing building in front of us. "You can still change your mind."

"That's not what I meant." I hold up my hands and laugh at the way they shake. "How many interviews have I conducted? How many interrogations?"

"I know I'm stating the obvious, but in all of those cases, you weren't speaking to the person who was convicted of your sister's murder. Don't be unfair to yourself."

"Still. You would think I would be able to handle it a little better without freaking out the way I am now."

"You're freaking out? That's how you would describe how you're feeling?"

"A little bit." Because why lie about it? This is Mitch. He's always been able to see through me.

And right now, what he sees makes him frown. "If you can't manage it …"

"I know. I don't have to do it. But I do. I really do." I stare at the building, too, while the clock ticks. I don't have much more time to sit here and second-guess myself. "I need to speak to him. I need to hear him. I need to know."

"What do you expect to find out?"

"I'm not sure. Who he is? Why they assumed it was him? Where he was when she went missing? Anything."

"I know you can do this." His hand closes around mine and stops the shaking. "I'll be right here. And if you can't handle it, come back to me. We'll go home. Sound good? You can do this."

"Thank you." He pulls me in and kisses my forehead, and once I've taken a deep breath, I open the door and step out onto the asphalt.

This is hardly my first time visiting an inmate, but the procedure is a little different now that I'm coming in as a civilian rather than as part of an active investigation. I go through all the steps—identification, personal inspection, before taking a seat in a hard, plastic chair along with another dozen or so people. Women, all of us. Two of them carry babies, and a third is doing her best to wrangle a pair of rambunctious toddlers. Twins, by the looks of them. I guess they're visiting a family member today.

All of us have a story. A reason we're here. From what I can gather by silently observing, it seems like I'm the only person who isn't here because they love the inmate they're visiting. I'm not carrying a homemade card or practicing my ABC's so I can show off when the time comes.

"Is this your first time?"

It takes me a second to realize the mother of the twins is speaking to me. "Pardon?" I ask.

She has an easy smile and a weary look around her eyes. "Your first visit. Is it?" She seems sweet and friendly, and I need that right now.

"Is it that obvious?"

"Just a little bit." She picks one of the little boys up when he holds out his arms, then settles him in her lap. Under his winter coat, he's wearing a cute set of overalls, and his dimples flash when he gives me a shy little smile.

"He's adorable," I murmur, wiggling my fingers at him until he laughs and waves his chubby little hand.

"Don't let him fool you. Most mornings, he wakes up determined to get on my last nerve." But there's a ton of motherly love in her voice. Soon, his brother decides he wants a little attention, too, and outstretches his arms for a seat on his mother's other knee.

"It's a long drive out here," she confesses. "And with my work schedule, I can only come out twice a month. But we make it work. You do what you have to do."

I have to wonder if Russell Duffy has anyone in his life who would go so far out of their way– and with two kids in tow, no less. From what I remember, he didn't really have a family. That was something the media played up, the absence of supporters in the courtroom. The only person who was there on his behalf with his attorney, and even then. I wonder what it felt like for him, going through something like that with nobody on his side. I'm sure there were plenty of people around town and beyond who took his loner status as yet another factor in his guilt.

The big clock on the wall slowly ticks off one minute after another, until finally, it's ten o'clock. At almost exactly when the hour strikes, the door leading beyond the waiting room opens.

"Alright, form a single file line." The guard hooks his thumbs into his belt loops and waits for us to get ourselves together. I help the young mother when the kids refused to be put down, grabbing her heavy shoulder bag for her.

What if he throws a fit once he realizes who I am? What if he refuses to speak to me? What if he taunts me? What was it Mitch said? I'm inviting trouble. I can't exactly help it. There are too many variables here, too many unknowns. I've never done well with the unknown.

Once we're all lined up, we're led through the heavy, metal door down a narrow hall whose white cinderblock walls glare in the light from the overhead fluorescents. The lights send a humming noise through the air that's loud enough to almost drown out the pounding of my heart. All these years, I've wished I could have just a few minutes with this man—though truthfully, in those fantasies we were alone so I could hurt him for everything he had taken from me. From my sister. Her whole future, and all the wonderful things she could have been. So many nights I spent lying in bed, wishing I could hurt him without repercussion.

And now, here I am, and the idea of coming face-to-face with him makes me want to run and hide. We never know how we're going to react in a situation like this, when we finally get something we thought we wanted.

The hall leads to yet another metal door painted a flat, cheerless shade of olive green. The guard unlocks it, then steps aside to let us file through.

The room is divided in half by a wall set with large, plexiglass windows. There are stools for each window and privacy dividers between each slot, and each slot has a telephone mounted to the wall. Just like in the movies. There's general chatter around me, but I sit silently with my trembling hands wedged between my knees in a vain attempt to keep them still. I wanted this for so long, and now I want to go home. What should I say to him? Why do I feel like I need to apologize?

There's no time to get my thoughts together before the door on the other side of the divider opens and the inmates begin filing in.

Too late to turn back now.

21

It's like watching the past and the present overlapping as Russell Duffy approaches the scratched plexiglass partition between where I'm seated with the rest of the visitors and the row of chairs on which inmates sit. He isn't the way I remember him, not at all. I might not have gone to the trial, but I sure made it a point to get a look at him outside the courthouse when I was supposed to be in school.

Another example of how everybody was willing to give me a pass during that particular era of my life. I skipped a lot of days and nobody bothered to inform my parents. I'm sure they didn't want to add more stress on top of an already painful situation.

The man I remember was skinny, drawn, unhealthy. His dark hair hung in snarls around his sunken cheeks and hid his eyes—except for once, one time when he happened to look across the street while being transported from the van that had brought him to the courthouse. One time when our eyes met. I've never forgotten that moment when an icy finger skated up my spine. Wondering if he knew who I was. If he would kill me, too, given the chance.

The man who sits across from me is twenty years older. He's also added some meat to his tall frame, but it looks good on him. He isn't a walking ghoul anymore. His once dark hair is now touched with snowy white and trimmed neatly.

It's the look in his eyes that's changed the most. That cold, hate-filled expression is gone. It's been replaced by, of all things, warmth that seems genuine.

Once he picks up his receiver, I do the same. "Hello," he offers, paired with a faint smile. "I have to say, I was surprised when I heard you wanted to see me. I never guessed you would."

"That makes two of us."

He even laughs gently, kindly. "You might not believe this, but I'm happy to see you. Really. I won't be offended if you don't feel the same. I understand."

I'm at a complete loss. This is not the man I expected. It's definitely not the reaction I expected. Twenty years have changed him, and not the way I would've imagined. Prison is supposed to harden people, isn't it? The man I locked eyes with outside the courthouse was hard as a diamond and just as cold. This guy? I wouldn't think twice about him if I saw him walking a golden retriever in the park. He'd fit right in.

"How … are you?" It's the only thing I can think to ask. It sounds pitiful, empty, not to mention awkward.

He doesn't take it that way. "I'm doing well." Holding the receiver between his ear and his shoulder, he folds his arms on the tabletop like he's settling in for a chat with an old friend. "And to tell you the truth, that's something I've been wanting you to know. You and your family. I'm doing well in here. If anything, my life has improved tremendously."

"How so?"

"When I was arrested, I could barely read. No, really," he insists when my eyes widen. "I knew the basics. But I dropped out of high school in the tenth grade, and even before that, I barely passed by the skin of my teeth. I'm pretty sure my teachers passed me because it meant getting rid of me, pushing me off on somebody else. I can't say I blame them."

I've witnessed way too many suspect interviews and have sat through far too many performances to question whether a person is putting on an act or showing me their authentic self. And Russell Duffy is sincere. There is nothing remotely false or calculated about him.

"You sound pretty intelligent. Educated."

His grin widens to a smile. "I've been taking classes. I got my GED—after first testing at a fourth grade reading level, by the way. I moved on to college courses after that. I recently earned my bachelor's in English Literature."

I'm reeling. If he'd come out wearing nothing but a thong and a clown wig, I wouldn't have been more surprised. "I'm glad to hear it. Really. What made you choose English Lit as your major?"

"Books ... are an escape." Just for a moment, his smile slips. I can only imagine he's thinking about the other side of prison, where everything isn't sunshine and rainbows and online classes. "That was where my love of literature began. Nobody ever told me how easy it is to disappear into a book. You can visit an entirely different world. You can be anybody, all thanks to the words of an author. It was like ... have you ever seen *The Miracle Worker*?"

"The story of Helen Keller?"

"Right. There's this scene at the end where Helen finally puts it together that things have a name. All the letters her teacher has been signing into her hand mean something when you string them in a certain order. And it's the turning point in her life. That's sort of how it was for me. I never knew I didn't have to be who I was. The way I was."

"And how were you?" He arches an eyebrow at my sudden question. "Sorry. But I was so young. I never heard anything about you."

He sighs, and for the first time averts his gaze. He's not smiling anymore, either. I'm afraid I might finally have pushed him too far.

"How was I?" he murmurs. "That's an easy one to answer. It's just not easy to say it out loud. I don't like thinking about the man I was back then. I grew up in a broken world. My parents were junkies, their friends. Their friends' kids were the kids I grew up with, and we all sort of picked up the habit. It was normal for us. It was all we knew. I realize that's no excuse."

I remain silent in favor of letting him feed my curiosity. I've wondered for so long how he ended up the way he did. What made him who he was. He could very well be the reason why I chose my career. Why I wanted to figure out what makes the human mind work.

"When we're young, we think our world is the world," I offer.

"That's right. That's exactly it. And we thought the people who worked hard and studied and held jobs were suckers, you know? We had the answers. We started stealing cars, robbing houses. I started dealing as well as using. Getting arrested and spending time in jail was a rite of passage." His sigh is heavy with regret. "I'm not proud of who I was."

His eyes meet mine, and something passes between us. I can almost hear his thoughts. And I know what's coming. There's part of me that doesn't want to hear more, but the rest of me knows this is what I came here for. We were never going to get through this visit without talking about her. The ghost binding us together.

"I know you won't believe me," he slowly murmurs, "and I understand. But I didn't do it. I was guilty of a lot of things back then, and there's nothing I can do to make up for anyone I hurt. There's not enough time spent in prison to make up for the things I did. But I did not kill her. I never even met her."

Of course, that's what he would say. That's what anybody in his position would say, even someone who seems to have grown and developed as a person over the years behind bars. Some killers don't confess until the very end, when they're moments away from a lethal injection for instance. When there's nothing left to lose and they want to continue into the next life with a clear conscience.

That's not what this is. I feel it. The way he doesn't avoid my gaze, and in fact seeks it out with his dark, soulful eyes. He's not running away from the truth.

I have to tighten my grip on the receiver or else risk dropping it now that my palms are sweating. "Why did they think it was you? Why did they arrest you for it?"

"I had a record. I was bad news. I was driving around town in a stolen car when they pulled me over—so arrogant," he adds with a gentle, regretful little laugh. "What did I think I was doing? Parading around, practically bragging about my crime. I was high, drunk, and there was merchandise I planned to sell in the glove box. And it just so happened I wasn't far from the place where your sister was found. I didn't have an alibi for when she disappeared, and it so happens I spent most of the weeks before then nursing a break-up with one of the few girlfriends I ever had. For me, that meant spending my waking hours either high, drunk, or both. I hardly showed my face outside, and for once I wasn't in jail. I couldn't prove my innocence."

He sits up a bit straighter and shrugs with a sigh. "It was a big case. The kind of case where everybody wants justice served right away. No doubt the police and the prosecutor wanted to wrap it up and put everybody's mind at ease. I hardly remember meeting with an attorney, to be honest with you. I was a scumbag who was getting what he deserved. I don't blame them," he insists when the ugliness of the scenario he's describing makes me wince. "I needed to be taken off the streets."

"But ... If it wasn't you ..."

"I would be dead by now." He says it like a man who's thought this over many times. "I know I would. Eventually, I would've crossed the wrong person. A lot of the guys I ran around with in those days are already gone—I get word around here, I hear things. I was going nowhere. Now, I've had the chance to become a whole person. I hope one day, I get my chance before the parole board so I can tell them so."

"Two minutes!"

We both look up at the announcement shouted out by one of the guards on his side of the glass. "Is there anything else you want to know?" Russell asks when he turns back to me. "I'm an open book."

I'm having a little trouble with the lump in my throat, so at first I settle for shaking my head. "Thank you for sitting down with me. It's meant a lot ..." *I don't think you killed my sister. I believe you.* "I wish ..."

"I wish, too," he murmurs. "But what good does it do? I am still very sorry for what happened to her. And tell your dad," he adds, "that there're no hard feelings. Really, there are not. I understand."

I can only nod, and I know there are tears in my eyes and I wish they weren't there but I can't help it. I'm sure he's right, that the direction his life was going in would have killed him by now if he hadn't changed his ways. That doesn't make it any easier to watch him being led away again, wearing the same orange jumpsuit as the rest of the men.

He even forgave Dad for shooting him. None of us ever asked for forgiveness, but he offered it eagerly. He's had a lot of time to think things over, I guess. Plenty of long, empty nights going over the whole ugly situation in his head.

Mitch is waiting for me out at the car. I've never been so glad somebody decided to take a road trip with me, because I am not sure I could handle all of the conflicting emotions battling it out in my head and my heart without him. I leave the room in a daze, following the other, more experienced visitors, moving without thinking. I need Mitch. I have to get to Mitch.

And then I step out into the cold, and he's there, getting out of the car once he spots me. Something about my face or the way I practically flee to him makes him open his arms, and I walk straight into them before burying my face in his neck. And now, it's safe to let the tears flow.

22

"I don't know what I expected, but it wasn't that. He was so... kind and warm and understanding."

"Prison might have been the best thing that could've happened to him," Mitch muses while digging through his salad. "I know it sounds harsh, but the proof is there. He needed to turn his life around somehow."

"He was so articulate. I didn't expect that, for sure. It's funny. Almost twenty years have passed since the trial, but in my head ..."

"You saw him the way he was back then. Of course you did. It's only natural."

"I don't know. I feel sort of silly now."

"Because you're much too hard on yourself, but that's nothing new."

"I guess." I stare down at my own salad, aimlessly picking through the lettuce. "Why did I order a salad?"

"Because I did, and I guess you didn't feel like making a decision." He chuckles at my forlorn expression but takes pity. "How about we get you something else instead? It's a long drive back to Broken Hill. Can't have you fainting for lack of nourishment."

"If you wouldn't mind, could you drive back? I have too much going on in my head." I feel like a little kid again, plain and simple. Lost and hurting and wishing I could blink my eyes or wiggle my nose like in the old TV shows and magically make everything better.

"Of course, I can drive. Hey," he adds, leaning in. "You got through it. You faced him, and you got through it. You are so incredibly brave."

"I don't feel very brave right now, but thank you."

"Well, you are," he insists in his usual, sweet way. "I'm proud of you."

"You're going to make me get emotional in the middle of a Panera."

"Oh, no." He gasps and touches a hand to his chest. "Not that."

"Always with the wisecracks."

"I'll stop making wisecracks when they stop making you smile." He sets his knife and fork down. "You know what I'm going to ask, right? I don't actually have to come out and say it."

"No."

His brows jump in surprise, and right away he sputters. "Oh. You don't? Sorry, I—"

"I was answering your question," I explain. "The answer is no. I don't think he did it. I would seriously doubt he had anything to do with it even without Maddie's picture and information on that cabin wall. He was very honest about himself. There's no self-delusion going on, if you know what I mean. He's not going back and revising the past. He faces it head-on. It probably sounds nuts, but I respect that."

"It doesn't sound nuts. I respect him, too. He knows who he was, he knows what he did. Why lie about it now?"

"Plenty of people do," I point out as I spear a piece of chicken and a slice of apple. Really, the salad is very tasty. I don't have the heart to enjoy it right now, is all.

"But he didn't."

"No. He didn't."

"And you believe him."

"I do. He was a lot of things, but he wasn't a kidnapper, and he wasn't a murderer. He got railroaded–which I have suspected for a long time as it is."

"There was no way he was going to get out of that without a conviction," Mitch surmises. "Not a case like that. Not with all that media attention."

"Exactly. What a nightmare that must've been. Can you imagine? Being accused of such a terrible crime, knowing nobody believes you when you say you're innocent?"

"It's unimaginable."

"But he's not bitter about it."

Mitch shakes his head. "I think I would be."

"I think most people would. In prison for something they never did, totally railroaded by everybody that had anything to do with it. But a lot of time has passed. I don't doubt he cursed us all back when he was convicted."

There's a moment of silence between us as we eat, while chatter and soft laughter rings out around us. It's strange, sitting here, talking about something so heavy while so many people are enjoying a nice lunch on a cold but brilliantly sunny day. Russell Duffy can't do this. Neither can my sister or any of the other girls whose deaths were documented in the cabin.

"What are you going to do next?"

Mitch's question pulls my thoughts back to the present. "I wish I knew."

"Are you going to tell them?"

There's no need to ask who he's talking about. My parents have been at the forefront of my thoughts all this time. "I feel like I should, but I don't have the first idea how to approach the topic. Hey, dad. Remember that guy you went to prison for shooting after he killed Maddie? Guess what? I don't think he did it. I think you shot him for no reason at all."

"Not exactly the sort of thing you want to talk about during a father-daughter visit."

"My biggest fear …" A pair of girls plop down at the table next to ours and I lower my voice, because let's face it, this is not the sort of conversation I want strangers to overhear. "Is that it will set him back. Both of them, him and Mom. They're finally getting their lives together. They're healthy, they're in recovery. Do I open Pandora's box and hope nothing too terrible comes pouring out?"

"Let me ask you another question. Are you going to go deeper into this? The case, I mean. Or will you let it go here?"

I don't need to think about it. The answer is obvious. "I can't let it go. He could be out there searching for his next victim now, whatever his real name is. I can't turn a blind eye and, like, hope he wakes up one day and decides he doesn't need to kill anymore."

"That's exactly what I thought you would say, but it makes sense." I meet his gaze before his mouth pulls up at the corners in a cheerless smile. "I think you have your answer. You should tell them. You have to warn them before you start digging into the past."

"I know I need to do it. But at what cost?"

"And what's the cost if you don't? We both know the answer to that one—you already said it yourself. It's unlikely this guy's going to wake up one day and change his ways. And even if you aren't the one who reopens the case, it will be reopened, and they will still deserve a warning so they can prepare themselves for having everything dredged up again."

"I know. I just wish it didn't have to be this way."

"So do I."

"It's going to break Dad's heart."

"I know that, too. I know you don't want to hurt him. But if Maddie's ever going to get real justice, we can't pretend there's nothing wrong with the way the case was handled." His eyes light up, seemingly out of nowhere. "Hey, it could mean getting an innocent man out of prison. I'd say he's paid his debt for whatever else he did back then. That's a big deal."

"One thing at a time," I implore with a half-hearted laugh. "I don't have the first idea how I would go about getting him out. I'm sort of flying by the seat of my pants here."

"It's a nice seat."

No matter how I fight it, I can't help grinning. "You cannot miss a chance, can you?"

"No, ma'am." He picks up his cup of lemonade and raises it my way in a mock toast. "I've still got years of lost time to make up for."

So does Russell Duffy, not to mention anyone else who may have gone to prison for the crimes committed by the man we know only as Andrew Flynn. Because this is about more than Maddie, and I can't allow myself to forget that. For all the pain my family has endured, every picture on that wall represented another family who went through it, too. There could be another dozen Russell Duffys out there serving time while a monster roams free. And when I think about it that way, I can't imagine not pursuing this. All of those girls deserve justice. Not only my sister.

Now, it's a matter of figuring out a way to break the news to my father without breaking him. I'm no closer to coming up with an idea by the time we finish our lunch and toss out the trash.

Mitch sees the strain I'm sure is written all over my face and slides an arm around my waist as we head out the door. "There's one good thing, you don't have to do any of this right away. Give yourself a little time. You'll know when it's time to break the news."

"You're right. I don't have to do anything today."

"What would you do without me?"

I know he's joking, but that happens to be a question I've asked myself a lot lately. What would I do without him? What did I do without him? Right now, with my heart so bruised and my brain grinding slowly with so much weighing on my mind, the idea of not being able to literally lean against him as we cross the parking lot is unfathomable. It makes me grab for his hand and rest my head on his shoulder.

"Right now? I don't have the first idea," I confess before sliding gratefully into the passenger seat so he can take driving duty.

23

I was always planning on heading to the station after my prison visit. There's too much work to be done and not enough time to get it done in, for one thing. For another, I'm a workaholic. I'm starting to accept the idea. As far as I know, the captain is scheduled off today, so at least I won't have to avoid him and the pointed questions I know he'll ask. Such as when I have scheduled my appointment to meet with Dr. Kenny. That weight is at least temporarily lifted off my shoulders when Mitch parks in the lot beside the station. "I should stop in at the store," he announces once we're out of the car. "Are you going to be okay?"

"I'll be just fine." And right now, I don't care if anybody's watching from inside. Let them watch. In full view of the entire world, I cup the back of

Mitch's neck with one hand and pull him down for a kiss I mean with all my heart.

When we come up for air, he releases a soft whistle. "What was that for?"

"For being you. Does there have to be any other reason?"

For one second, he's the kid I used to know. Blushing a little, wearing a lopsided grin as he brushes windblown hair away from my face. "I wanted to be sure. Don't work too hard. You've already had a long day." He's right, but the day is not over yet. I can't afford to let my personal business slow me down.

And once I'm in the station and checking my messages, I know I made the right choice by coming in here today. One of the messages is from the field office, and I return the call before I've even had a chance to take off my coat. "This is Agent Forrest," I report. "There was a message for me to call in? From the forensics department."

The switchboard operator transfers me and moments later, I'm connected. "Yeah, we wanted to let you know we uncovered a handful of IP addresses."

"And this is a good thing?"

"It's more than a good thing." There might as well be a duh at the end for good measure. "It's a huge break."

They seem to be sure of themselves, so I won't point out that an IP address is not the same as a name. But it is a start. "So what are we looking at?" I ask as I take a seat at the desk.

"The locations are fairly widespread. There are even a few we tracked to Asia and Europe."

"What about something more local?" I cross my fingers, praying silently for something I can use.

"There are dozens all over the country, but three in the northeast."

"And that's all of them? You track down the addresses for all of the transactions?"

"Unfortunately, no." My heart doesn't have time to sink before he adds, "This is only the last month's worth."

Only a month. So many purchases, in only one month.

Once I push past that realization, my scalp starts to tingle. If someone purchased footage from the Duncan's cabin and took a liking to Cayden—I hate thinking about it that way, but that's the general gist—it means one of those three northeastern locations could be the one linked to the man who tried to shoot me in the woods. "Please tell me at least one of them is nearby."

"As a matter of fact, all three are within a couple of hours of Broken Hill. Now, we can't trace these addresses to an individual, but we can trace them to their locations. One of them happens to be a library twenty minutes outside of town, according to Google Earth. The other two are residences a little further out."

I can barely think with my gut screaming at me that this is it, this is the break I needed. "And exactly where would I find these locations?" I grab an envelope from the top of the desk and scrawl the addresses on the back.

After looking them up online, it makes the most sense to visit the library first. It's closest, for one thing, and I'm hoping there are security cameras that will give me a look at who might have accessed their computers at the time the transaction went through. I didn't get a look at that man's face, but I remember his shape clearly. I see it every night when I close my eyes, after all.

I CAN'T COUNT how many times Mom and Dad scoffed at the idea of me or Maddie being able to research a school project in the comfort of home.

"Back in my day, we had to go to the library. If we wanted to make a copy of something, it cost five cents per page." They wore it like armor, those memories. Warriors recounting the olden days. I'll never forget asking Mom what happened if the information they found in an encyclopedia was outdated. You would think I'd committed blasphemy or something similarly serious. "If it was outdated, who was going to know? The teacher couldn't Google it." Good point.

I might not have needed the library for school research, but I haunted Broken Hill's public library. It didn't take long for Dad to realize I would bankrupt the family if he kept buying new books for me. One day, he took me to the library. I got my first library card, and I was off and running after that. I knew the librarians by first name, and sometimes they would set aside new books they thought I would enjoy rather than putting them out on the shelves for everybody else to get the first crack at them.

And that was back during the good days. In the not-so-good days, the library was my refuge. I would find an empty corner and lose myself in a fantasy rather than face cold, hard reality.

This isn't the Broken Hill library, but that doesn't keep me from smiling in fond remembrance as I enter. There's nothing like the smell of a library. All those books, some of them so old, old enough that they carry the scent of the past. It's a beautiful, old-fashioned building with ceilings that stretch up for what seem like miles over my head and tall windows that allow beams of light to shine down on the stacks. The floor, the tables, the woodwork along the walls—all of it is carefully polished. There's a lot of love around here.

Nobody would ever guess what has gone on at one of those computer terminals further back in the room. I see them over there as I approach the desk and I make it a point to study the four people currently huddled over the keyboards. Three women and a teenage boy. Well, there's nothing wrong with hoping, is there?

"Can I help you?" A woman who looks to be roughly my mother's age looks up from her computer and offers a warm smile that reminds me so much of childhood, it's like a hand gripping my heart. I've never met this woman before in my life, but she symbolizes so much. I wonder if there are any kids around here right now in the same position I was in back in my youth. Running away, hiding.

After introducing myself, I get to the point. "I'm investigating a case out of Broken Hill. A little boy was kidnapped down there recently. Maybe you heard of it."

"Oh, that poor little boy?" Her head bobs up and down while her thin lips twist in an expression of horror. "Yes, I saw that on the news. Do you think somebody here had something to do with it?"

"To tell you the truth, I'm not sure yet if what I am here to investigate has anything to do with it at all. But we do have reason to believe that there was video footage of the cabin in which that boy and his family were staying, and someone using one of your computer terminals purchased that footage according to the IP address discovered by our forensics department. At the very least, I need to get a look at this person, because whether or not they drove down to Broken Hill, they committed a crime by paying for the footage."

"While they were here?" She's completely scandalized. If she wore pearls, she'd be clutching them as she gazes up from her chair in horror.

"Do you use any sort of keystroke software on these machines?"

The utter confusion etched across her face answers that question easily enough. "I'm not sure I understand what you mean."

"That's alright." Trying another direction, I continue, "I have a date and time the footage was purchased. Do you have security cameras here in the library? I need to take a look at the man or woman who used the terminal."

"I'm sorry. We have a camera trained on the front door but don't have any at the computers. A privacy issue, you see. In case someone is accessing personal information, we're not allowed to capture that on camera. I think it's silly, personally—how am I supposed to read someone's bank password from a distance? But…" She trails off with a shrug.

"I see." I grit my teeth and do my best to maintain a pleasant attitude, even while screaming in frustration inside. A dead end. Once again. I could take a look at the footage from that day and see if anyone entering or leaving the library matches the general size and shape of my shooter, but unless I know for sure who did and did not use a computer that day, it would be the same as chasing my tail. I've done enough of that already.

All I can do now is thank the woman, then leave with my tail between my legs. I still have these two residences to check, but it's late enough in what's already been a very long and emotional day that I decide to return home, instead. I can always try again tomorrow, and when I do, I'll make sure to have backup with me.

Because if I do happen to stumble upon the home of the man who killed Cayden and tried to shoot me, I doubt he's going to welcome me with open arms.

24

Dr. Stella Kenny works through the Portland field office, treating the agents involved in situations like the one I faced during the blizzard. It's a better idea for me to drive most of the way to Portland than it is to drive down to Boston.

And as I sit in her waiting room, where I've been assured she'll be ready to see me in only a few minutes, I have to wonder if any of this is going to help. Not that I feel I need help, but I'm not entirely deluded. I need to work through what happened that night, and not only to me. Granted, the shoot-out itself would normally be considered plenty of reason for a cop or an agent to speak with a doctor. That's typically how it's done.

It's just that I don't have much patience for what's typically done.

Yet none of that is the doctor's fault, which is why I offer a genuine smile when the door leading into her office opens. "Agent Forrest?" she asks in a soft, warm voice. "How nice to meet you. I'm Dr. Kenny."

I don't know if she's doing it on purpose, or if she simply happens to be a warm, maternal sort of figure. I couldn't explain why that's my first impression even if someone forced me to try. Maybe it's the floral perfume she wears, and how it reminds me of something Mom used to wear years ago. Maybe it's her gentle smile, the way she covers my hand with hers when we shake in greeting. It could be the thick, cozy cable knit sweater she wears. Whatever it is, I feel myself loosening up. My apprehensions are slipping away.

In other words, the woman is good. She's very good. And we haven't started our session yet.

"Please, come on inside. I'm sorry I kept you waiting – I had an emergency call regarding a patient of mine. But everything is worked out now."

She ushers me into her office, and I can appreciate the care she put into making it as warm and cozy as she could. "This is lovely," I tell her as I look around a room decorated in shades of brown, gray, and deep orange. More warmth. More comfort. She takes a seat behind a large, walnut desk and gestures toward a deep, plush sofa sitting beneath a windowsill covered in small plants that lend a cheerful look to the space.

"Thank you for the compliment. I spend a lot of time in here," she points out with a gentle laugh. "I figured I might as well create something comfortable and welcoming."

"I'm sure your patients appreciate it."

The warmth in her gaze seems to deepen as she regards me once I've sat down. "I hope you don't mind my looking through your records prior to the session. I like to understand as much about a visitor as possible before we get started. I find it saves time, and I know time is always of the essence. Especially when you're in the middle of a case."

When I lift my eyebrows, she chuckles. "Hey, I started off the way you did. Got my doctorate, applied it to my work with the Bureau. I was a field agent for years before I went into practice. Now, I'm still serving the Bureau, just in a different way."

"Then you understand the pressure."

"All too well, Alexis." She tucks sandy blonde hair behind both ears and clears her throat, signaling the end of the *getting to know you* phase. "Now. Why don't you tell me about the reason you're here? What brings you in to see me?"

"I was bullied into it."

She releases a tiny laugh. "That's fair. Plenty of people are. But why were you bullied into it? What was the precipitating event?"

The thing is, I'm sure she knows. If she's looked into my background, she's already aware. I'm sure by now there's been a note of the shooting entered into my record. "I was involved in a shootout while searching for a kidnapped child the night of the big storm."

"A terrible storm. And you were out there in it?"

"I couldn't go home and hunker down when there was a nine-year-old boy out there somewhere. I had to do my best to look for him."

"And?"

"And it was too late by the time I found him."

"But you did find him."

"I did, and I came close to the individual I believe was responsible. Why else would he have been out there? And why else would he have taken a shot at me?"

"Makes sense. You were uninjured?"

I nod. "Physically, I'm fine. I finally managed to get warm again."

"And internally?" she gently prods. "How are you feeling?"

"Like I didn't do enough. I wasn't there in time."

"I'm sure you were not the only person who searched for that boy."

"No, I wasn't."

"The last I checked, Broken Hill has a solid police force."

"Yes. That's true."

"Then why does all of this sit on your shoulders? Why not rest in the knowledge that you gave the family at least a bit of closure? Even if you couldn't capture the perpetrator then and there?"

"Because he's still dead. That poor little boy. It's going to tear his family apart."

"And how do you know that?"

"Because that's what happens, isn't it?"

She draws her lips into a thin line and pauses before responding. "Is that what happened to your family?"

She's done her research. "Yes. It is."

"I'm sorry," she murmurs. "I didn't ask that question as a way of throwing it in your face. I'm sure you understand that." I nod mutely. "But you know, while we can assume that couple is going through the worst thing a parent can experience, that doesn't mean the past will repeat itself."

"I understand that up here." I tap the side of my head. "But it's not so easy to convince the rest of me."

"I understand." And the thing is, it seems like she truly does. She gets it.

And because she does, my apprehension starts to melt away. My tongue feels looser. "I should know better than this. I'm not exactly unfamiliar with the human psyche."

"Don't be unfair to yourself. I know, it's easy for me to say, and I won't pretend there haven't been times when I've held myself to the sort of rigid standards you hold yourself to. But it's unfair to expect so much from yourself. You are only human, and you have more than your share of personal experience with tragedy. It's only natural you would want to spare others the pain your family suffered."

"And then ..." I snap my mouth shut before anything else can come out. I'm not here to talk about Maddie or my family. That's not what today is about. It's about filling a requirement and getting the captain off my back.

"What were you about to say? Self-censoring isn't going to do you any favors. I hope you know that."

This part isn't so easy to talk about. "I feel selfish, bringing up my own past."

"But that's what we're here to discuss. I expect you to talk about what you've been through and how it informs your work. What's on your mind?"

I'm suddenly extremely uncomfortable on this deep, soft sofa. "I have ... a lot of personal issues bubbling up right now. I never expected it. But ... I have reason to believe the man who went to prison for my sister's murder is innocent of the crime. And now, I need to decide if and when to tell my parents I went to visit him. My father doesn't even know I found anything to do with Maddie."

"I see. You don't want to bring it all back."

"Exactly. That's exactly right."

"What you have to remember is, you can't hold yourself responsible for the emotions of others."

"I know that already."

"But do you?" She peers at me from over the rims of her glasses. Her expression is unreadable. "You said it yourself. You can know something up here ..." She taps her temple the way I did to mine. "But it's another story, making your heart believe it. Until you do believe it, you're going to keep pushing yourself as hard as you have been. You might even take risks like going out into a blizzard alone to search for a child in hopes of sparing a pair of strangers the same agony your parents experienced."

When I look away, embarrassed at being seen so clearly and so easily, she lets out a motherly sigh. "And you were lucky this time, which I'm sure you know. But what happens next time you're driven that hard? You can't punish yourself like this and still serve the public the way I know you want to."

"But if I didn't go out there, who would?"

"Is that how you see life? If you don't do it, who will?"

I want with everything in me to avoid the question, because I see where she's going. And as good as it feels to speak to someone who not only listens, but can relate, there's still part of me that needs to be right.

"Yes," I finally admit in defeat. "That's how I feel."

"And where do you think that comes from?"

It takes no time to come up with an answer. "When my needs weren't met when I was a kid."

"Because of your family's tragedy."

"Yes. I understand now that I had to do everything for myself. That sort of instilled a habit in me. I'm the only person I can rely on."

"That's natural. But is it true, or is it a story a little girl told herself years ago?"

I blow out a big sigh, puffing my cheeks, before chuckling. "You really know how to cut to the heart of things, don't you?"

"It's sort of my job." We share a laugh. "And you know the answer. I know you do. Life doesn't have to be the way it was in the past, but if you don't do the hard work of breaking out of old patterns, you're going to see the same reality pop up again and again. And as I described, you're going to keep taking risks that you might end up regretting."

"It's not easy for me to sit back and let somebody else do the work."

"Nobody's saying you have to take a backseat. I'm only strongly suggesting you take it easy on yourself and start identifying situations in which you feel that drive start to build in you. Telling you to go, push, work. No matter how tired you are, no matter how many other people there are who could help carry the load. Do you think you can learn to slow down and identify those pivotal moments?"

"I have to, don't I?"

"Nobody has to do anything," she reminds me. "But I do think it would be in your best interest if you give it a try."

"I'm going to do my best."

Her proud smile shouldn't make me feel as good as it does. I must've needed it. "I believe you."

25

I have spent more time in my car over the past several days than I have in the past month before them. At least I'm seeing a lot of the state, which happens to be very beautiful even with the absence of leaves and the constant, sometimes breathtaking cold. There are still plenty of lovely moments, such as when an early morning sun paints the bare treetops a glorious shade of gold that's almost distracting enough to make me forget I'm driving.

"Just be careful, alright?" Concern rings out in Mitch's voice, filling the car through the speakers connected to my phone through Bluetooth.

"I will. They're sending me a squad car for backup when I arrive. I'm not going to take any big risks, don't you worry."

"Newsflash, I'm always going to worry."

"Newsflash, I'm always going to appreciate it."

"Remember what the doctor told you."

I know he has only the best intentions, but that doesn't keep me from rolling my eyes just a little. What was that about appreciating his concern? "She said a lot of things. Don't make me regret telling you about our conversation."

"Don't take any unnecessary risks. You don't have to be Super Agent all the time."

"I'm only going to ask questions of this guy, whoever he is." According to the information I pulled up once we had an address tied in with the IP address from Forensics, the house is rented by a man named Charles Nelson. The only problem is, there is no trace of Charles Nelson living in the area. If the house has a landline, it's not under his name, nor are the utilities.

An eerie sense of overlap plagues me — after all, we're in a similar situation with my guy in Broken Hill. The name he provided Hawthorne Academy when they hired him was nothing but an alias.

It couldn't be the same person, could it? What are the chances? And why would he run the risk of going down to Broken Hill when he knew we were on to him? Otherwise, why would he have run off all of a sudden? He could've come back to check in, to watch the activity around the cabin ... but why risk capture by kidnapping another kid? Why wouldn't he settle for flying under the radar, feeling superior? Like a deity on high.

Isn't that exactly how I described a voyeur to the captain? Watching everything from a distance, like a deity. Enjoying a sense of power. I need to be careful, or I might start jumping to huge conclusions that won't help anybody. Finding ways to connect the two men and muddying everything up in the meantime.

Naturally, my thoughts wander toward my personal life. My family. Maddie. Russell. I should tell Dad soon. If it turns out the man I'm currently on my way to question is the same as the handyman I let slip through my fingers on the grounds of Hawthorne Academy, I might end up wishing I'd had a conversation with Dad before now. I would hate having to rush through something like that for fear of him hearing it from somebody else. *Hey, did you hear they think they caught Maddie's actual killer?* I shudder to think what that would do to him.

I have to settle for telling myself it won't be that simple. This won't be the same man.

But that doesn't stop me from preparing myself just in case it is.

It's wishful thinking, and it's not going to get me anywhere. Instead of reveling in fantasy, I need to figure out next steps when it comes to Russell. Since a case like this is never as easy as the killer breaking down and admitting their guilt, I will need to find evidence. A bunch of photos and articles in a cabin is not the same as concrete proof.

Where do I go from here? I should ask for help, the way I know Dr. Kenny would tell me to do if she knew what I was thinking right now. Even though I have a connection to the case, that doesn't mean I have to do everything by myself. In fact, that's exactly why I shouldn't.

But after twenty years, what are the odds of finding anything that could link Andrew Flynn or whatever his name is to Maddie's murder? I'll have to start from the beginning, I guess. Look at the original evidence. It will hurt—I have no doubt of that. I can't afford to worry about it. And I'm sure the doctor would have a field day with that response, too, but it doesn't change how I feel. I'm not going to step back and wash my hands of this because of a little discomfort.

GPS tells me I'm a couple of miles from the remote house by the time I pull to a stop and place a call to the local police station. "We'll have a car out there for you in five," the dispatcher assures me, and I thank her before ending the call and waiting. If I were going to describe the home of the sort of person who would buy illegally obtained footage off the dark web, I would probably start with a location like this. In the middle of nowhere, surrounded by forest, with very few intruders. I guess there's a reason the clichéd image of a pervert huddled over his computer in the middle of a sad, remote little house exists.

It's only four minutes before a squad car pulls in behind me. I step out to find a young man climbing out from behind the wheel. He may only have started shaving yesterday for all I know. "Agent Forrest," I tell him, extending a gloved hand.

"Joe Schaeffer." I can't stop staring at his baby face as we shake hands—and when I find him frowning, I'm embarrassed. "I graduated from the academy three years ago," he explains with a good-natured chuckle. "I'm not as young as I look."

"I'm sorry," I tell him, laughing at myself. "I'm sure you get it a lot."

"No. You're the first one." But he grins and I decide I like him.

"So, do you know what we're looking for here?" I ask. "Who we might be dealing with?"

"Yeah. I got the full rundown. And you think this guy might be the one you tangled with down there?"

"It could be. We can't discount the possibility of him being dangerous."

"Do you think you would know him if you saw him?"

That's not an easy question to answer with confidence. "How about I wink at you if I recognize his shape and size are the same as what I saw that night? This way, you'll know to keep an eye out for him. He could have a gun in the house."

"I like to assume there could be a gun in the house either way."

"Good thinking." I appreciate how seriously he seems to be taking this. "Alright. Let's head on over. I'll take the lead." We climb into our vehicles and he follows me up what could be considered a driveway but is more like a path worn into the earth after years of wheels rolling over the ground have created deep ruts. Mr. Nelson, if that's his name, has been back and forth quite a lot. Though there is snow on either side of the car as I navigate the narrow passage, the ground beneath my tires is only wet. He's been through here plenty since the storm.

If my suspicions are correct, he wasn't home that night. And people think I'm the one who takes risks? He must have known there was a blizzard on the way, but he couldn't help himself. He had to make the drive all the way to Broken Hill.

If this is the man. I have to keep that in mind, but it helps to get a feel for who we might be dealing with. Someone obsessed enough, they would ignore the danger and head out anyway.

It's like we're two sides to the same coin—if this is the same guy.

The house sits roughly half a mile from the road. Its siding is old and grimy, but nothing a pressure washer couldn't fix. The roof has seen better days, as have the shutters on the windows. White, now a rather dingy gray. The place is small, compact, and I wish I had come up here with Schaeffer in my passenger seat rather than letting him roll up in a patrol car. The front yard is visible from every window at the front and along the side of the house. Someone accustomed to privacy would naturally notice the sound of an approaching car. He could be looking out the window this very second for all I know, plotting.

It's too late to think about that now, as we both park our cars and meet between them before heading up to the front door. The house backs up onto a thick, dark, expansive wood. There isn't a sound anywhere except for that of our breathing and our footsteps in snow that's now mostly ice after days of melting under the sun and refreezing.

I step up to the door and knock, straining my ears for anything coming from inside. "Tire tracks lead around to the back of the house," he observes in a tight whisper.

Another knock, and once again, there's nothing but silence in response. I knock again and I'm about to suggest we check around back to see if the car is even there.

When all of a sudden, it's not so silent around here anymore. It takes a moment for me to realize the sharp crack coming from inside is that of a gun being fired.

Wood chips explode from the door and almost in the same moment, Schaeffer goes down. I drop to my knees, staying low in case another bullet crashes through the door. He is still conscious, blinking rapidly, gasping for air and covering his stomach with a hand that's turning red as if by magic.

Somewhere, there's a sharp bang that has nothing to do with a gun. Only when I hear a car engine do I realize the shooter ran out the back door. I've barely had time to process this before a dark blue vehicle flies at full speed around the side of the house, kicking up dirty snow in both directions.

"Stop!" I scream, pulling my weapon and aiming, but it's already too late. He's already lost in the trees leading back down to the road.

Instinct leaves me desperate to get behind the wheel and chase him down, but that would mean leaving

Schaeffer here. Instead, I pull up my phone and dial 911 while unzipping his jacket. A dark red patch is growing across his abdomen, soaking into his shirt. "I'm ... gonna die, right?" he whispers. Already, he's so pale, like the color in his freckled face is draining into his abdomen and pouring out.

"You are absolutely not dying today." When a dispatcher answers, I bark into the phone. "Officer down! I need an ambulance out here immediately!" Somehow I manage to remember the address off the top of my head while pressing hard against the wound in Schaeffer's abdomen.

"You'll be okay," I tell him, the words tumbling from my lips before I think about them. "You'll be just fine. Hold on."

While the man I am now sure was behind Cayden's death gets away.

26

"He should be alright," one of the medics assures me as he closes the doors to the ambulance. "Lost a lot of blood, but they'll get him patched up at the hospital."

"Thank you." Some of that blood is still on my hands, literally, even though one of the medics was kind enough to pour a bottle of water over them so I could rinse off the worst of it.

The area is crawling with cars now as the local police converge on the scene. The crackling of radios and the commotion of overlapping voices fills the air and threatens to make my head split in two. I should be out there. I should be chasing this guy down.

Instead, I've ordered roadblocks and checkpoints and that's all fine and good, but I know what I saw. I know who I'm looking for. I didn't get a clear look at the man, but the bulky shape behind the wheel is burned into my memory.

It's him. The sort of man who shoots first, then asks questions—if he sticks around at all. Twice now, we've brushed against each other. Twice, I managed to escape with my life.

Frankly, I'm starting to take it personally.

The fact is, no matter how much I want to be out there, I need to process the scene. Now that Joe Schaeffer has been taken away, I can turn my attention to the house at my back.

"We have every car in the area out there and plenty of eyes." A rather grizzled officer falls in step beside me. "You know how it is. One of us goes down, everybody takes it to heart."

"No doubt. How are we on the search of the woods in case he decides to hide out there until things calm down?"

"We've got a group of hunters coming in to back us up and cover every inch of the ground if that's what it takes. Nobody knows these woods better than they do." It's good thinking. And this is a small area. There might not be the sort of manpower available in bigger towns like Bangor or Portland. Any extra body they can gather is a plus.

"Let's take a look inside." I lead the way, careful of every step even though we've already gotten the all-clear from members of the bomb squad who were sent out to confirm there were no explosives planted anywhere. I can't afford to assume anything, that much is clear. We're dealing with a desperate man who has a penchant for letting his gun do the talking.

The first word that comes to mind when I stand in the center of the living room is *sad*. This is a sad little place, sparsely furnished, with bare walls and sagging furniture that stinks of grease and smoke. There's a TV opposite the sofa, propped up on an old end table that looks like somebody let their dog gnaw on it.

"Not exactly something you'd see in a magazine spread," someone remarks as they pass through.

"Do we have any confirmation of this guy's name yet?" I look around, hoping to find a piece of mail or something personal that might have a name on it, but the small stack of junk mail sitting on the arm of the rough, plaid sofa features no fewer than four different names. None of them are Charles Nelson.

"Sure," the older cop offers. "It's either Keith or Larry or Susan or Mike." He tosses a sales flier to the floor and mutters a curse. The energy around me is extremely tense, and it's not like I can't relate. But I didn't almost lose one of my own today.

For the most part, the officers moving in and out give me a wide berth while they dust for fingerprints. As much as I crave a hint of the guy's real name and where he might hide in an emergency, what I want most now is evidence of his computer crimes. Something to tie him directly to Cayden.

There's no computer in the living room. I move on to the eat-in kitchen and find roughly what I expected after what I've seen so far; outdated appliances covered in grime that a simple cleaning spray would clean up, plenty of clutter on the counters, a sink full of unwashed dishes on which mold has begun to grow. The trash can is crammed full of empty takeout containers and paper plates. Why wash the dishes when you can simply buy new ones and toss them when they're dirty? He would've done himself a favor by emptying the sink into the trash while he was at it.

There's no laptop in here.

My next stop is the second floor, then, where a pitifully empty bedroom featuring an air mattress and a pile of dirty clothes both saddens me and turns my stomach a little. He lives like an animal, which tracks. After all, he is one.

The only other option besides the bathroom — I'm not going in there, no way — is a second bedroom. At one time, it might have been considered a home office. There's a desk in front of a window overlooking the woods behind the house, a wheeled chair whose leather covering is cracked and split in countless places.

And a desktop computer. My heart skips a beat and my pulse picks up speed. Finally. A break. Even though I'm sure the files will be enough to turn my stomach and make me wish for the power to go back to a time before I viewed them, they'll be enough to connect him to Cayden.

Or so I wanted to believe.

Right away, I realize the problem. The computer tower sits beneath the desk, where the side panel has been removed and set aside. And something is missing.

"What is that?" One of the officers points to a metal box sitting beside the dirty keyboard.

An average cop might not recognize it, but I can identify it at a glance. "It's called a degausser." I approach slowly on heavy feet. He must have been ready for this. The time between our vehicles approaching the house and the shot he fired through the door was all it took for him to slither through my hands.

"What's a degausser?"

"It's a machine that can erase the contents of a hard drive in roughly five seconds." I shake my head, then turn toward the window and look out over the dark, bare trees stretching out as far as the eye can see. "He wiped his hard drive so we can't access anything he stored on it."

"But you can, like, send it to the Bureau and they can recover it, right?"

The hope in his voice is an anchor attached to my already sinking heart. "I'm afraid not. Whatever was on there is gone now. The hard drive is garbage."

And we're no closer to catching this man than we were before.

27

Nightfall has a way of making everything seem spooky and foreboding. In the distance, beyond the house where I've spent half the day, the occasional flash of light tells me the hunters are still searching every inch of ground for signs of the man who may or may not be named Charles Nelson. We're still unsure of that, though police are currently running down any leads based off the name. Something tells me they're chasing their tails, but it's not for me to tell them how to do their jobs. Cops have a way of resenting people who do that.

"We got a hit on the car registered to this address." Sergeant Baker's voice is tight with fatigue and strain, but there's hope in it when he finds me standing in the front yard. "A 2010 Honda Accord."

I close my eyes, trying to bring up a mental image of the car that sped through here. "It could easily have been an Accord," I agree, but that's about as far as my memory will take me.

"At least we have something to look for." He makes a call to keep a lookout for a car with that description while I fight to stay upright. Even stepping out into the cold, clear, night didn't help shake the cobwebs from my brain. It's been a long day. Longer than most, even. I watched a kid fight for his life and came frighteningly close to losing my own. The weight of that has begun settling over my shoulders, pushing down on me, leaving me with heavy feet and a heavier heart. I've had enough close calls to last a lifetime.

And now, hours later, my empty stomach growls and my weary head wants nothing more than a pillow to rest on.

"Hey, there. You alright?" Sergeant Baker looks at me in alarm before taking hold of my shoulder. "You looked like you were ready to go down there for a second."

"Did I?"

He treats me to an assessing gaze before giving me a firm, grim nod. "You should go. There's not much more you can do here tonight, and you look like you're ready to drop."

Usually, I appreciate brevity. Not when it's offered with what sounds like dismissal. He must see the reaction his statement brings on and understand it for what it is, because the deep brackets around his mouth soften along with his steely gaze. "You're not doing yourself any favors by working yourself to death. And you had a close call earlier. We'll take it from here, at least for now. Go get some rest."

I don't have it in me to fight the idea. Rest is what I need now more than anything. Well, maybe not more than anything, since I could use a pair of strong arms and maybe a firm chest thrown into the mix. Something to rest against. Something to hold me up when I'm weak and weary.

We make plans to catch up in the morning, and I get behind the wheel with a sigh of relief before groaning softly. The cold has not done my body any favors—my muscles are sore and stiff, and I'm sure some of that has to do with tensing up all over when the gun shot rang out. I've been achy and slightly miserable ever since the adrenaline wore off, though I managed to ignore the discomfort by keeping busy. I have nothing to distract me now.

It's only six o'clock. There's plenty of time to get back to Broken Hill, if I want to. The problem is, the case is here. Charles Nelson, if that's his name, is here somewhere. Unless he drove back down to Broken Hill, I'm not going to find him there. It would be better to stick around, at least for the night, and now I wish I had considered that before driving out. My head falls back against the headrest and for one agonizing moment, I am as close to bursting into tears as I've been in a long time.

"Looks like I need a hotel," I mutter with a sigh before opening the browser on my phone. I don't care about star ratings or anything like that. So long as it's clean and won't require too much driving, I'm there.

As it turns out, my phone rings before I get too far into my search. Yet instead of making me smile the way it normally does, seeing Mitch's name on the screen makes my heart sink. I have kept him somewhat up to date on what's been going on all day, and the intention was always to meet up tonight. Now, sitting alone in the car with his name in front of me, I miss him more than ever. He won't like hearing sadness or fatigue in my voice, though, so I make it a point to sound a little more cheerful when I answer. "Look who it is. Just the guy I was thinking of."

"I'm flattered. You haven't called to say you're wrapping things up, so I assume you're still at the house."

"I am in the process of looking for a hotel room. I'm sorry," I add in a rush. "I'm too tired to drive back, and besides, I want to be close by when they find him. I'm sorry."

"You have nothing to apologize for. And it just so happens I know a place you can stay."

I sit up a little straighter, staring out the windshield and watching a handful of officers milling around. "What place is that?"

"I'll send you the address. Trust me. You'll like it." And with that cryptic little sendoff, he ends the call. A moment later, I get a text including an address, as promised. When I tap on it and open the Maps app on my phone, I find a hotel eighteen minutes from where my car currently sits. Did he rent a room for me, predicting this would happen?

Reality is even better than my best guess. When I pull into the lot in front of a five-story hotel that looks like it's mainly used for business travelers passing through, I find a familiar car parked near the doors to the lobby. Right away, tears of relief fill my eyes, and it takes me a moment to let the emotion run its course. Once I've stopped blubbering, I call Mitch back. "Where are you?"

"Room 417. There's a feast waiting up here for you—and I'm not only talking about myself." With renewed energy I get out of the car and hurry out of the cold and into the warm, inviting lobby. Everything seems brighter now, somehow. Better.

And once I reach room 417 and Mitch opens the door, I throw my arms around him. It's enough just to hold him.

"I hope you don't mind." His breath is warm against my ear, but not as warm as his arms. All the parts of me that were dark and sad and hopeless are filled with light now.

"Mind?" I press my nose to his shoulder and inhale deeply. His spicy, musky scent is far better than the sour, greasy stench of that depressing little house. "This is the best surprise I've had in forever."

"Good. I was hoping you would see it that way." He sets me on my feet and closes the door while I peel off my coat. "Also, I figured you could maybe use a change of clothes. You left a few things at my place. I've been keeping them there for you."

My heart stutters. "You were keeping clothes at your place for me?"

"It was either that or throw them out."

"And there I was, thinking you were being romantic." Once I've kicked off my shoes, I hug him again and this time pair it with a kiss. "Thank you. Thank you so much. This is exactly what I needed. How do you always know what I need?"

He lifts a shoulder, wearing a funny little grin. "I don't know. I guess I think about you a lot."

Before we can take things any further, he clears his throat and eyes the cluster of white cardboard containers on the dresser. "Come on. I ordered practically the entire menu at the Chinese place down the road. Hopefully it's still hot enough to eat."

It is, though I would eat it anyway even if it was cold. I'm that hungry, and the food is that good. "They got a call from the hospital about an hour ago," I tell him while digging through a container of fried rice. "The kid should be okay."

"What a relief." There isn't much relief in his voice, though. When he looks at me to find me staring at him, he frowns. "I'm sorry, but you have to know where my thoughts immediately went."

"But I'm fine."

"Yes, luckily. You are." Then he waves his hands, shaking his head almost violently. "Nope. We're not doing this. I told myself we would not do this."

"For what it's worth, I didn't think I was taking a huge risk by going out there today. But there's always a possibility somebody's going to do something wild."

"I know. I don't have to like it."

"I'm sorry. You have to know the last thing I ever want to do is worry you."

"I know." He gestures to the dumplings in front of him. "These are great. If you want any, you better take one now before I empty the whole thing into my mouth."

"Like in the old Garfield cartoons?"

The sound of his laughter is balm for my soul. "Wow, come to think of it, I don't like Mondays, and I do love lasagna. Maybe we have more in common than I thought."

It's nicer to laugh like this, so that's what we do. We laugh our way through dinner, then through a comedy on TV while cuddling in bed. I'm asleep before it's over, and when I wake up in the middle of the night with the TV off and the room dark, I'm still tucked firmly against Mitch's chest. I can't think of anywhere I'd rather be.

28

I'm wrapping up my call when Mitch steps out from the coffee shop, holding a steaming cup in each hand and a paper bag tucked under one arm. "I see. Alright, I should head back to Broken Hill for now. But I'm never more than a phone call away."

"And you'll be the first person I reach out to when we hear something new. Until then, all we can do is hope this guy shows his face somewhere." I can only agree before ending the call and groaning in frustration.

"Everything okay?" Mitch asks, handing me my drink before fishing out a breakfast sandwich wrapped in parchment paper.

"Sure, everything's pretty much where it was last night. They haven't seen the car anywhere, they haven't found him in the woods. He's somehow managed to fall off the face of the Earth."

"He'll pop up. He has to." He sounds awfully sure of himself as he pops the lid of his cup before taking a sip. "It's weak," he declares, wrinkling his nose.

"You're just a snob," I giggle. Then I take a taste of my own drink and realize he's not wrong. Still, it's good coffee, and hot enough to chase away the chill of a frosty morning.

"Are you driving back?" he asks as we stand between our cars.

"I'll be right behind you," I promise – before something tugs at my heart.

And he sees it. "What's up?"

"I was just thinking about Dad. Every day, he's on my mind. I keep telling myself I need to talk to him about Maddie and Russell, but I keep finding reasons to put it off."

"Maybe you need to get it over with, get it off your mind for a little bit. You're not doing yourself any favors by putting it off."

"I know. It's eating me alive."

"Don't do that to yourself." His kiss tastes like coffee and bacon. I can think of worse things to taste on his lips. "I say get it over with. Rip off the Band-Aid.

Frankly, it's probably a small miracle he hasn't heard by now about what you guys found in the cabin. There's bound to be a cop in town who hears about it and tells him. It's been a long time, but everybody knows about the shooting."

"I know." Boy, do I. "And you're right. It would be cruel, leaving him to find out that way." The thought of that firms up my resolve and stiffens my spine. "Rather than drive straight into the station, I'm going to go see him. And then maybe I'll have a nervous breakdown."

"You know I'll be there for you if you do." And that's the thing. I do know that.

"How come you're so good to me?" I ask, standing on tiptoe to kiss him.

"It's easy to be good to you. Especially since I know you're not always good to yourself."

"So, what? I'm a stray puppy you've taken under your wing?"

"It did sort of sound like that, didn't it?" We laugh together before he shakes his head. "No. Not at all. You are Alexis Forrest, and I've been wanting to take care of you for most of my life."

I don't know what to say. Maybe there's nothing to be said. Maybe it's enough to kiss him one more time before we get in our respective vehicles and begin the drive. He's certainly given me a lot to think about, and even that is a blessing since it distracts me from the dread of what I know I have to do.

"Well, isn't this a nice surprise! My hero daughter has come to see me."

There's something about the way he says it, and the unbridled joy in his words takes me back. I never quite appreciate how much I miss his constant, unwavering support until I'm with him and he reminds me of what I've missed all these years. When I was little, I would sometimes roll my eyes – the man always knew how to lay on the praise. I didn't always feel like I deserved it, like he was going overboard.

"How are you doing out here?" I ask after giving him a hug.

"Oh, just fine. Made it through the blizzard without any trouble. Helped a couple of the neighbors—you'd be surprised how many people never consider checking to be sure their generator has gas until it's already too late and the power's out and they're snowed in."

"I'm sure you're a hero to those people."

"Speaking of heroes ..." He trails off as we enter the trailer. "I got word through the grapevine that my daughter went out there in the middle of that blizzard."

"I had to do it."

"I know it felt that way. I only hope you're not taking too many risks. I know you're devoted to your job, but not at the risk of your own life, sweetie."

"I know." I take off my coat and place it on the sofa before sitting beside it. I'm so jittery all of a sudden, and my hands shake until I have to hold them between my knees to keep them still.

"Are you alright?" He sits in his chair and eyes me warily, but with concern. "You seem worked up."

I couldn't ask for a better segue. Yet somehow, I can't find my voice. Everything I told myself on the way here repeats in my head. He deserves to know. It's better to hear this from me. I'm doing him a favor. Yet I can't force the words out. I can't find my voice at all.

"Honey? What is it? Is it your mom? Is she okay?"

"Mom is fine." At least the question shook me out of my silent indecision. "But I did come here with something I need to tell you."

He leans forward, his gaze intense. "You're not sick or anything, are you?"

"I'm fine. Really, it's nothing like that." Somehow, he doesn't look relieved. I can understand why. I'm not exactly making this easy. "So, you remember I originally came to town to look for Camille Martin when she went missing."

"And you found her." A smile stirs at the corners of his mouth. "Like I said. My hero daughter."

"I was in the right place at the right time—but that's not important now. I ... rather, we ... found the cabin out in the woods where the kidnapper held Camille until she escaped. It was about as grim and disgusting as you would imagine. There was a lot of information there."

His head tips to the side as he reaches for the Diet Coke sitting next to his chair. "Information? What do you mean?"

"Maybe that wasn't the right word for it. There was a lot of ..." This is not going well. I can't find the right word. I know how I would describe it to a cop or a fellow agent, but he's neither of those things. I don't want to shock him too much. "There was what we are taking as proof of other crimes he committed, whoever he is. Camille and Leila weren't the only two girls he ever kidnapped. That's what I'm trying to say. He had a bunch of photos and articles and things like that all around one of the rooms. And even though we haven't found him yet for questioning, we have to conclude for the time being at least that those articles and photos represented past victims."

"Oh, you're kidding. Out in the woods? How does a person do something like that with nobody ever finding out?"

Good question. "I don't know, honestly. The cabin itself was practically falling apart. It might've been an old hunting cabin at one point, and this guy was just squatting there. But that's not the point. That's not why I brought it up."

He's clueless, searching my face, his thick brows drawing together. He's worried about me, that's all. He hasn't jumped to any conclusions because in his mind, the man who killed his little girl has been behind bars all this time. There's no reason for him to think about Maddie.

I really hope I'm not about to make an unforgivable mistake.

"Dad. I wanted to tell you this before anyone else got the chance. I've been in that room, where he had the pictures and everything. And ... Maddie was there. I'm sorry, Dad. But I saw it myself. I saw her on that wall."

Slowly, realization begins to dawn. He sits up straighter, his throat working. His eyes start moving around the room, while his mouth moves soundlessly.

"I'm sorry," I tell him again in a soft voice. "We don't know anything for sure, yet, but—"

"Are you saying you think this guy killed Maddie? Is that what you're trying to tell me? You think Maddie's killer has been out there somewhere all this time?"

"Yes, Dad," I tell him while his face slowly crumples. "That's what I'm saying. I think they got the wrong guy."

29

The kettle whistles on the stove and I take it off the heat, pouring water into a pair of mugs. I was glad to find tea bags in the cabinet. We could both use something hot and soothing right about now. My father has sat still as a statue while I acquainted myself with his kitchen. Every so often I steal a glance without making it look like I'm staring. I don't want to hover. He needs space and time to figure out how to feel.

"Do you want sugar?" I ask, holding up the small canister. The question stirs him from his thoughts long enough for him to give me a quick, distracted nod.

"Here you go." I hand him one of the mugs then sit down with my own, holding it between my hands to keep them warm. It's not exactly cold in here, per se, but it's not toasty, either. No wonder he's wearing a thermal shirt beneath his V-neck sweater.

He takes a few sips of the tea before setting the mug aside. "I'm sorry for sort of … going away for a minute. That was the last thing I ever thought I'd hear."

"And I am so sorry to drop it in your lap that way. I've been worried somebody else would tell you about it. I didn't want you to find out that way."

"Always worried about your old man." A ghost of a grin floats over his face, almost like a butterfly that only lands for a second before fluttering away again. "I know it couldn't have been easy for you to find that, but you've been worried about me."

"It's what I do. I worry."

"So." He clears his throat before scrubbing both hands over his short hair. His way of resetting. It's nothing more than an absentminded habit, but seeing him do it unlocks profound longing in my heart. What I wouldn't give to go back for just one day … "What's next? I assume you'll pursue this."

"Of course. Nothing could stop me."

"Do you know anything so far?"

I hate to shake my head, but I'm not going to lie. "Nothing yet. The blizzard sort of slowed things down, made it difficult to get out there and continue working the scene. And then there was Cayden—the little boy who went missing. But I'm not giving up on this." I was about to say I'm not giving up on Maddie, but I'm not trying to jump to any conclusions—at least, not in front of him. I've already jumped to countless conclusions in my mind.

"Plus," I continue when all he does is stare at the floor, "it looks like he's used aliases all this time. It's a matter of finding out which, if any, is his real name. But the Bureau's working on it. From what I understand, they took the evidence to the field office in Portland. So the top people are on this. And just as soon as I can get out there, I'm going to go. First, we're trying to catch the guy who kidnapped Cayden, but we're very close." And yet I don't feel like I'm doing enough. I'm certainly not giving him any peace of mind.

"Does your mother know?"

I nod slowly. "I told her. She thought I should wait until we had more evidence before coming to you. But like I said, I was afraid—"

"I understand." He gives me a wary look, like a man who is about to ask a question but is unsure whether he wants to hear the answer. "How many others? You said they were all over the walls. Did you count how many there were?"

"Thirteen in all."

He squeezes his eyes shut like he's in pain. I suppose he is. "So many."

"I'm sure all of the cases will be reopened. I don't know anything yet about the outcome of any of them. I've been sort of busy."

"You aren't the only FBI agent in the world, Alexis."

"I know. But I feel like I should know more about this by now."

"So you don't know anything about the other families? Who these kids were?"

I think I understand where this is coming from. Whether or not he's consciously aware of it, he wants the assurance that Maddie's case wasn't the only one that resulted in an arrest and a conviction. He wants to believe this sicko, whoever he is, was only documenting crimes without having any involvement in them. He wants absolution. Some shred of hope to hang onto. I wish I could give it to him.

Instead, all I can give him is the truth as I currently understand It. "The last I heard, we were able to confirm three of the cases he documented. They were all teenagers, all girls. One of them died by strangulation." He winces and his jaw ticks and I know he's thinking of Maddie. We both are. "But another was stabbed, and the third was shot. So there's not really a pattern, which could lend itself to a theory that he's obsessed with these crimes, but had nothing to do with them. They could be unrelated."

He picks up his mug, snickering softly before blowing on the surface of the liquid. "But …"

"But … he did have all of the information. Almost like he was collecting trophies. And considering he brought one of his victims to the cabin and held her there as he was strangling a second …"

"You don't have to go any further. I understand what you're trying to say." He sets the mug down, but not without splashing a little of the tea on his wrist thanks to the way he still trembles. "You're telling me I shot the wrong guy."

My heart is going to break by the time this is over. "Dad …"

"That's what this is all about. I know. But they were so sure." He pounds his fists on the arms of his chair and I jump at the sudden flash of emotion. "They told us so! They had the guy, had him dead to rights. How did they convict him if he was innocent?"

"I don't know, Dad. I want to find out. I'm going to find out. I swear."

"I trusted them! And the prosecutor, the police who arrested him, I trusted all of them. We all did. Now you're telling me there's a chance they pulled this guy off the street at random?"

"I'm really not sure of exactly what happened. but I'm going to find out. I am. I can't let this go."

I don't know if he hears me. He's too deep in his pain, far beneath the surface where it's dark and isolating. "And he's been sitting there … all these years …" He bends at the waist, his head in his hands.

I slide off the sofa and onto my knees in front of him. "Listen to me. I went to see him."

"You what?" His head snaps up, eyes wide and wild. "You saw him? When?"

"On Sunday. I drove out to the prison and I spoke to him."

"I can't believe he wanted to speak to you. After everything …" He releases a broken sob, and it's a knife to my heart.

"Dad, please believe me. He's not who he used to be." He turns his face away, struggling and failing to hold back his broken sobs. "He would be dead by now otherwise, and he understands that."

"I shot him. I shot him, honey. I threw … I threw it away … It wasn't him?"

"You don't have to feel guilty. He said he understands. He said he doesn't blame you. He ... He forgives you for it."

"And he said he didn't do it?"

"Yes. He swore he never met her."

"But tell me." His red eyes dart over my face. "Tell me the truth. Did you believe him?"

It's a single word. Three letters. Yet somehow, I can't force it out. All I can do is nod, then wrap my arms around him and hold him while he cries.

"What did I do?" he moans before a wracking sob tears through him. "I threw it all away, and for what?"

"I'm sorry. I'm so sorry." That's all I can say, though it doesn't feel like it's enough. I doubt anything could feel like it was enough at a time like this. All I can do is hug him and be here.

And after that? After that, I find this man.

I find him and I put him away forever.

30

As much as I didn't want to wait another day to drive to Portland, I'd already spent two hours driving to Broken Hill, then another few hours with Dad to make sure he was going to make it through the shock I delivered. By the time I left, it was too late to consider heading out to the field office for information on what I've come to think of as Maddie's case even if it's not. Instead, I went to Mom's and was glad she was too busy showing a house and attending a networking event to be home. I needed the time with my thoughts. For one wild moment, I considered going upstairs to Maddie's room. I was that deep in my memories. It almost seemed like a good idea to touch the things she used to touch before good sense finally won out and I put myself to bed.

Now, I show my credentials before stepping through the lobby of the Portland field office, then taking the elevator up four floors to where Special Agent Jeremy Childs is heading up the investigation into the cabin's contents.

Immediately upon meeting Agent Childs, I get the sense of a man who decided a long time ago he didn't have the time or the patience for pleasantries. "It's about time," he mutters when I enter his office. "What took you so long to come in and see me?"

I'm a little thrown by his brusque attitude. Rather than shake my hand, he stands behind his desk with his hands on his hips, peering at me through narrowed eyes that I'm sure have seen it all over decades in the bureau. He's somewhere in his fifties, maybe closer to sixty, with thin, gray hair and a toned, athletic body.

"Well?" he prompts. "I've been waiting for the meeting with the agent who discovered all this information, yet this is the first time seeing you. There's a decades-old serial killer out there."

Somehow, I find my voice. "You'll have to forgive me, Special Agent Childs. I've been in the middle of investigating the disappearance and eventual murder of a child back in Broken Hill. I've been crisscrossing the state for days, and it is still an active investigation. But I want very much to be actively involved in this case."

Because one of the dead girls is my sister. Right, like that announcement wouldn't get me thrown out of his office on my ear. I might as well say goodbye forever to any chance of being part of the case if I admitted that.

I get the feeling he's put off by my explanation. He wanted a reason to be annoyed with me, and now there is none. "I see. Well, at any rate, you're here now. And considering we're dealing with thirteen potential victims of this guy, whoever he is, we need all the eyes and hands and brains we can gather to work on this."

"Please, whatever I can do." I glance around his office, then at the cubicles beyond it where busy agents and staff work without paying attention to us. They must have heard him dressing me down thanks to the open door. I guess they're used to it. "Is there … I mean, can I …"

Finally, he takes pity on me. "Do you want to look at the evidence we pulled from the cabin? Is that what you're trying to ask, Agent Forrest?"

There's something about him that makes me feel like I'm back in school, being stared down by a teacher. Like there was a project due today and he's exasperated with me for not getting it done. I need to remind myself I am an agent, too, not a child to be chastised or spoken down to. "I would like to. I haven't seen it since I was inside. Then the blizzard hit, and everything got moved out here."

"Sure. Everything was left in a room down the hall. All the clippings and the photos, along with just about everything else in the cabin." He leads me from his office down the hall, and I practically have to jog to keep up with his long strides. He's a no-nonsense kind of guy, and I appreciate that. This is the kind of man who gets things done, and that's what I need. It's what Maddie needs. It's what my parents need.

He opens a door and flips on the light, and at first I am overwhelmed by the stacks of boxes lining three walls. They're stacked five boxes high. This is not a large room, so the effect is even more overwhelming. "Oh. This is …"

"It's a lot," he agrees. "Years worth. Not only that, but we managed to grab case files from several of the local police jurisdictions. You'll find those cases in boxes labeled with the victim's names. Otherwise, the rest of the clippings and such are organized in folders in the box labeled Miscellaneous."

"I see." And of course, right away I scan the boxes, looking for the name Forrest. I'm gripped by mixed emotions when I don't see the name—right now, in the moment, that's probably a good thing. I don't want Child to make the connection. On the other hand, I want to look through Maddie's file more than anything. But then I've already been through it, at least as much as I could get my hands on. I can't afford to lose sight of the other dozen kids involved in this.

"You want to be part of the case? Here's where you start. Dive in." With that, he's gone, already halfway down the hall before I can catch my breath. If anything, it helps me not take those first painfully awkward moments personally. That brusque, no-nonsense attitude is simply who he is.

I'm sure Mitch will be pleased to know I'm spending my day here, sifting through evidence. The worst I could get from all of this is a paper cut and maybe a headache after reading so much small print from so many articles.

Since there's no table or chair in the room, I pull a few boxes from one of the stacks to use as makeshift furniture, then perch delicately on top of a box full of papers – nothing breakable, just in case. I then open the first box in front of me and dive in as Agent Childs instructed. The box I've opened is labeled Blitzer, and taped to the inside of the lid is the blown-up, grainy image of a smiling girl with blonde hair and green eyes.

Cheryl Blitzer was fifteen years old in 1994. She was babysitting one night for a pair of twins who lived only two blocks from her family home only twenty minutes outside of Broken Hill. According to the statements from her parents, they assumed she would be safe walking home as she had done it so many times before, and the area was considered safe. Sadly, somewhere in those two blocks, someone pulled her off the street and into their car. She was found five days later, half-submerged in a drainage ditch clogged with fall leaves.

Sarah Wayne was fourteen in 1996. A couple of the girls on her field hockey team said they saw a strange, rundown sedan circling the field a few times before practice was called for the day. One of the girls noticed Sarah walking in the car's direction—but that was the direction she usually took to go home, so the girl couldn't say for sure whether Sarah was approaching the car, or simply happened to be walking toward it and planned to pass by. No one saw her get in. It was three days before they found her in a thick patch of overgrown brush running alongside railroad tracks not half a mile from her home. The photo in the box looks like it was taken from the school yearbook. She was pretty, fresh-faced, with a confident smile and gleam in her eyes. I bet she would've been a terror on the field.

But she wasn't strong enough to fight off the man intending to strangle her.

Seeing the faces and reading the names and learning about the girls ... all of it sits heavier on me with every lid I lift, every backstory I learn. The weight of it settles on my shoulders and sits on my chest until I find it difficult to breathe. So much grief. So much lost potential. In another case, Molly Jackson's supposed killer was arrested, tried, and convicted. He died in prison a few years later, killed by another inmate.

Was he innocent, too?

It's a couple of long, sad hours before I come to the box labeled Miscellaneous. That's where I find my sister, in a manila folder labeled Forrest. I pick it up gingerly, like it makes a difference, then flip the folder open and stare down at Maddie's wide, brilliant smile. All these years later, it's no easier to see her so full of hope, and life, and light. Somebody extinguished that light, along with so many others. And these are only the cases we know about.

Ligature marks around the neck… Skin beneath the fingernails, DNA test inconclusive. She fought, but the DNA they scraped from under her nails didn't match anything in the database. I'm sure that only helped the prosecutor's case. He couldn't prove it was Russell Duffy's DNA, but nobody could prove it wasn't. I have to turn the page before the more gruesome details of her condition can keep me up tonight. It's enough to know she'd been out there for a while, and nature had taken its course.

So many kids. I doubt anybody could blame me for feeling more than a little overwhelmed as I sit here surrounded by their lives and their deaths. Where do we begin? Where could he have gone?

And is he already hunting for his next victim?

31

"They have another pair of agents working on it," I explain to Mitch on my way back to Broken Hill after hours spent in that cramped little room, surrounded by the evidence of so much destruction. "And they know to keep me posted on any major updates while I'm away. I should try to get out here more often to keep an eye on things."

"But like you said, there are other people working on it."

"Mitch. I have to be part of it. I just have to."

"I know. You're about to run up the mileage on the car."

"You're not wrong."

"How are you feeling?"

"Frankly?" I ask with a dry laugh. "Like I got run over by a bus."

"I'm sure you do. Where are you? How far out?"

"Around an hour. Traffic's moving, so there shouldn't be any problems."

"Now that you've said it out loud, there will be."

"You're probably right. I probably jinxed myself."

"Just think, when you get back, we'll have dinner together."

"That sounds nice." So nice it warms me, body and soul. There's someone waiting for me. Someone who wants to see me. Who wants to hear about my day. I was missing that without knowing I missed it, living my empty little life in Boston. Granted, I would've taken offense if anyone had told me it was empty, because I didn't know. I had no idea it could be like this. Sweet and simple, easy. He doesn't ask for more than I can give, but that only makes me want to give him more. "What about you, sir?"

"Me?"

"Yes, you. We've done enough talking about me. What about you? How was your day?"

"It wasn't so bad. I had a woman complain her coffee was too hot."

"Was it?"

"It was as hot as our coffee ever is. I didn't microwave it or something to make it boil."

"Some people are never happy."

"Isn't that the truth."

"So what happened?"

"Nothing. She complained and demanded a refund, but once it was clear nobody was really paying attention—not even the people in line—she gave up and wandered off."

"Did you know her? Is she a regular?"

"I've seen her around town before. She comes in every once in a while."

"Who knows? That might have been her only contact with other people all week. Some people just want to be heard. They want somebody to pay attention to them and listen and care."

"Now you have me feeling bad for being irritated."

"It's not an excuse for bad behavior," I add with a laugh. "And I would not blame you if you told her to stick her coffee where the sun doesn't shine."

He barks out a laugh. "And she thought it was painful when she took it by mouth?"

"Exactly."

"Camille is due to come back in over the weekend for her first shift since ... you know."

The announcement jars me. "No kidding. I'm so glad she feels strong enough to start living again."

"And I promised her from now on, if she doesn't have a ride home, I'm driving her. No arguments."

"Something tells me she's not going to argue with you on that." After all, the last time she did, she was taken off the street by a killer. If it hadn't been for her courage and resilience, she wouldn't have made it out alive. Only the fact that she escaped and ran through the woods meant the difference between life and death.

"You should stop in and see her if you have the chance."

I see where he's coming from, but the idea leaves me wincing. "I'm not so sure. She might not want to be reminded of things."

"I see your point, but I doubt she could exactly forget. You know?"

I see his point, too. No doubt she carries the memories with her. Stumbling through the dark, not having the first idea where she was or whether he would find her. "How about we play it by ear?" I suggest. "I would like to see her, but only if she's ready for it."

"I can always count on you to be thoughtful."

"Coming from the most thoughtful person I know, that's quite a compliment."

"You're just buttering me up."

"Is it working?"

"Oh, like a charm."

"What else happened today?" I'm thirsty for his stories. He connects me to what is real. Of course, my work is very real, but it's also very dark and leaves me wading through some fairly ugly and heart-wrenching stuff. It's too easy to get lost in that.

Mitch is my light. He brings me back to what's true. What's good. If I didn't have him to look forward to seeing when I get back, what would I have to look forward to? I would probably head straight to the station and work until I fell asleep at my desk. Because what else would there be to stop me? What would be the alternative? A girls' night in with mom? Sure, the idea is nice, but it's not something we could do every night.

Mile after mile ticks away on the odometer, while Mitch treats me to one story after another so I won't feel so lonesome during my drive. Finally, he asks, "What do you want to do for dinner?"

And even that is wonderful. The fact that he assumes we're going to have dinner together. Like it's a done deal, like this is how it's going to be. That's how I want it to be—that much I know for sure. "I am open to suggestions. Maybe not Chinese since I'm still regretting gorging myself last night."

"How about a nice pasta and bean soup? I have the ingredients at home and can have it whipped up by the time you get here."

My mouth waters at the idea. "You say the nicest things, you know that?"

"I do what I can."

"You wouldn't happen to have some delicious bread lying around to eat with it, would you?" I cross my fingers.

"You might get lucky," he replies.

"Are you talking about the bread, or about other things?"

"You'll have to get here to find out."

"Careful, or I might have to put the pedal to the metal and break a few speed limits."

When the call is over, I switch the radio on and smile when an old favorite of Dad's fills the inside of the car. One of the oldies he used to play on the weekends while he was out working on something in the garage. I can almost see myself on the front porch, my nose in a book, while the music floated my way on a sweet, spring breeze. The call with Mitch and the promise of seeing him soon has done wonders for my mood, because if it hadn't been for him, the song might have made me pull over so I could get a handle on myself. I feel so close to those old days right now, like they're on the other side of a veil. A veil so gauzy thin I can almost see through it. but I don't want to sweep it aside. I'm almost afraid to. I'm afraid of what's behind it. Like avoiding a half-healed wound for fear of making things worse.

When the phone rings again, I jump at the jarring sound piped through the car speakers. I don't recognize the number, but I don't have the luxury of being able to screen my calls, either. It could be something important. "This is Agent Forrest," I announce on answering.

"Sergeant Baker," the man barks. "We got a tip."

The hair on the back of my neck lifts until it stands straight up. "Tell me."

"The car registered under that address was spotted fifteen miles outside Broken Hill."

"You're sure?"

"A gas station on Route 1. 2010 Honda Accord, dark blue. A clerk called it in. They're sending units out there right now."

"Exactly where is it? I need a mile marker." I'm coming up on the exit for Route 1 as I speak. Normally, I would hang a right turn on reaching the bottom of the ramp. Instead, I swing left, because as much as I want to be with Mitch, I need to see Charles Nelson arrested. I need to see this through.

I want to look him in the eye so he knows he didn't hurt me.

I need to do it for Cayden.

32

By the time I arrive, there are squad cars all over the place, surrounding the gas station and the large convenience store sitting a handful of yards from the pumps. Right away, I notice the blue Honda sitting at one of those pumps, currently empty.

I show my badge on parking and getting out of my car. "Who is the officer in charge?"

"That would be me." A man who can't be much older than myself emerges from a cluster of officers debating on the plan of attack. "Murphy."

"Forrest. I've been looking for this guy. I'm pretty sure he took a shot at me in Broken Hill."

"He's wanted for the Cayden Duncan murder, right?" I nod, staring into the convenience store. The lights are off and the windows are covered. It's impossible to know what's going on behind the glass.

"He's a person of interest," I confirm. "Who also shot and nearly killed a cop when we went to question him on it. What's happening?"

"We got the call twenty minutes ago. The clerk at the store recognized the car from the APB description." He points to a truck parked close to the store's entrance, then to a second vehicle parked alongside the store. "From what we gather, he's barricaded himself in there with a clerk and the owner of the truck."

"And he's armed?"

"See for yourself." He jerks his chin toward the building and now I see the hole in one of the windows. "We tried to approach, and he fired on us."

Most of the glass is covered with ads—cigarettes, lottery tickets, two-for-one deals on twenty-ounce bottles of soda. He has the advantage of being able to peer out through small gaps between those ads, but we can't see inside. "What about the SWAT team?"

"They're on their way, but it could take another hour or more for them to get here. They have to come out from Bangor."

We might not have an hour. We might not have ten minutes. If he's agitated enough that he's already fired, there's no telling what he'll do next. "Anyone tried to speak to him?"

"That was the intent of approaching the building."

"I see." Thinking fast, I pull out my phone and let GPS track my location. The gas station appears and I tap on it, bringing up a phone listing. "I'm going to call."

"You sure about this?"

"I need to get a sense of what's going on in there. Whether the hostages are still alive." *Please, please, don't let me be too late.* I place the call and hold the phone to my ear, while Murphy signals for everyone to quiet down.

The phone rings once. Twice. I stare at the dark windows from behind a squad car, concentrating with all my might on somebody answering the phone. *Do it. Pick up. Talk to me.*

On the fifth ring, there's a sound. Someone picked up the receiver. I hold my breath, while holding up a hand to let the others know someone answered. "Hello?" I venture in a calm, even voice. "Is someone there?"

"Yes." It's a woman, and her voice is tearful.

"My name is Alexis," I tell her. "Who am I speaking to?"

"Jenny. My name is Jenny."

"It's good to hear your voice, Jenny. Can you tell me what's happening inside?"

She whimpers. "I... I don't think so."

"Is he making it hard for you to speak freely?"

"Yes," she squeaks.

"And does he have a gun?"

"Yes." She whimpers again—a shaky, painful sound. "Please, help us."

"Are you the clerk who made the call to the police?"

"Yes."

"That was very brave of you, Jenny. You did the right thing."

Another strangled whimper. "I don't think so."

"I know it feels that way now." I look at Murphy and mime writing on my hand. He digs through his pockets and pulls out a small notepad and pen on which I scrawl *negotiator*. He points to his watch and holds up ten fingers once, then twice. Twenty minutes. I might not have twenty minutes at this rate.

"I would like to speak to him. Can you tell him that? Can you put him on the phone?"

"I'll try." I stare intently at the windows while a brief, muffled conversation goes on inside the store. Please, please, work with me here.

All at once, the tearful whimpers are replaced by heavy breathing. He doesn't say anything at first. He only breathes into the phone. "Who is this?" I ask.

"You know who it is. That's why you got all those cars out there. Don't play games." His deep voice is tight, strained. Dripping anger.

"I promise you, I'm not trying to play games."

"Then let me go. I want to get out of here. I want you to let me go, or I'm gonna blow their brains out. Both of them."

"It doesn't have to come to that."

"And it won't, if you get everybody out of here so I can go. Do you want to know my demands? That's my demand. I want all the cars gone, I don't want any helicopters overhead, I want to be left alone. Understood?"

"I understand."

"Good. Get it done!"

"I need you to promise me you're not going to shoot those people. They didn't do anything to you. You don't have to shoot them."

"Then get out of here!"

"I'm afraid that's not a fair exchange."

"Then I'll blow them away now!"

My heart seizes at the determination in his screams. "Let them go now, and there's no reason for us to hold you here. Let them leave. Once we have them, we'll go. You have my word."

"And what good is your word? I don't know you. You don't know me, and you're not my friend, so stop talking to me like you're trying to convince me otherwise. Got it?"

"Got it," I murmur as evenly as I can. I have to pull him back from the ledge before he loses what little control he has. "Let's both calm down. This doesn't have to end badly for anyone. But I need you to stay calm, and not give anybody a reason to fire into the store. We don't want anybody to get hurt. Is everyone alright in there now?"

"Yeah, they're fine."

"Good. That's good. See? So long as they're alright, we have no problems."

"Then why'd the cops show up in the first place? I know they've been looking for me. Don't act like you're gonna let me go, because I know you're not."

"In a situation like this, a deal can be struck. That's what we're going to do. But I need you to let them go. Nobody here wants to hurt you. They only want to ask questions."

"Yeah, right. I'm sure that's all they want."

He has no idea who I am. He doesn't know it was me he tried to shoot during the blizzard, that it was me standing outside his front door when he fired through it. He doesn't know I know exactly why the police want to speak to him. I decide to keep it that way—he might only become more agitated if he knew about our special connection. "We're going to get through this, you and me."

"You and me?" He barks out a bitter laugh. "There is no you and me. Stop trying to get in my head!"

"I assure you—"

"Screw your assurances!" He slams the receiver down, and the call goes dead moments before gunshots erupt, shattering yet another window. I drop to a crouch behind the car along with the officers standing nearby, and we wait out the barrage before everything goes quiet again.

Think, think! There has to be a way to get them out of there and get our hands on him without getting anybody killed in the process.

All I have to do is figure it out.

33

"We have a problem." Murphy heaves a heavy sigh, staring at the store after getting off his phone. "The negotiator is stuck behind a pile-up on the interstate. There's no telling when they'll get here."

This is getting worse and worse with every passing minute. "And the SWAT team is still ..."

"It's going to take a while. Maybe longer than we have." He turns to me, and the men around him do the same. "Do you know anything about this guy?"

"I know one thing. He's a killer. And he's not stupid —he magnetically wiped his hard drive so there would be no chance of us recovering his files. He's good at covering his tracks. Savvy. At the end of the day, that's what matters most to somebody like this. Because he knows what will happen if he's caught.

He's desperate. He's a killer. Cayden Duncan might've been the first or he might've been the twentieth for all we know right now."

"Do you think he'd kill the hostages to get away?"

"I have no doubt of it. We can't risk going in there while he's still got hostages."

"So what do we do?"

That's the problem. I'm not entirely sure. At a time like this, all of my training comes back to me all at once. The only problem is, everything is swimming through my head at the same time, ideas bouncing off each other, images and warnings flashing in front of my mind's eye while a pair of innocent people could be taking their last breaths. It's one thing to learn how to approach a situation like this, but it's another to be thrust into it. They are real lives on the line here. Real stakes.

Slowly, an idea begins to emerge. It's shadowy at first, unclear, but it begins to solidify until finally, I turn to Murphy. "I have a crazy idea. I think it might work, but I need everybody to play their part." I explain to him the other insanity that's taking root in my mind—at first, he stares at me, while his eyebrows lift until they're practically merged with his hairline. "It might be our only shot at getting him alone."

"If you're sure you want to try this, we are right here with you." Still, he looks concerned as I redial the number for the store.

This time, Charles Nelson picks up on the first ring. It's easier for me to think of him using that name, even if I never use it. "What part of this don't you understand?" he barks loud enough that I have to hold the phone away from my ear for a second. "I'm going to kill them. I will paint the walls with their blood if those cars don't back off and let me drive away from here. What do I have to do to make you understand?"

"Nothing. We get it. We're going to leave."

Silence. I cross my fingers, exchanging a nervous glance with Murphy. "Yeah, right," Nelson snickers. "Try again."

"I mean it. Walk out of the store, and nobody's going to stop you from getting into your car. You have my word on this. All we care about is the hostages and getting them out of there alive and in one piece. If there are gunshots or any other signs of trouble in the store, all bets are off. Otherwise, you're free to go. All we need is a minute to get the cars out of here."

More silence, longer this time. I have to focus on controlling my breathing. I can't let him hear how frayed my nerves are, how scared I am for those people. How much is riding on what he decides.

"Listen," I murmur when he hasn't responded in far too long, "I don't know what this is all about. I don't know why the APB was put out. I do know this is going to get much worse for you if you hurt those people." Because I don't owe him any honesty. I'm too far from the store and half-hidden by a car—he can't see me clearly. He doesn't know we've met before.

"So you'll go? I can leave and nobody's going to stop me?"

I close my eyes and release the breath I was holding at the sound of hope brewing in his voice. "That's right. Nobody's going to try to stop you. You're free to go. Can I trust you? Can I trust you'll leave those people alone if we leave you alone?"

"Yeah. Yeah, you got a deal. But I want those cars gone now."

I give Murphy the thumbs up and he directs his officers to get in their cars. I then hand him my keys. He closes his fingers around them, and we exchange a look that lasts the length of a heartbeat but feels much longer. "Alright. We're going to start moving out here," I tell Nelson. "Just give it a minute, and we'll be out of your way."

There's a lot of motion, a lot of moving bodies, and I use that to my advantage. There's a pair of squad cars parked lengthwise between Nelson's car and the convenience store, and I use them as cover while slipping into the backseat of the Honda and quietly closing the door before stretching out in the messy, soiled backseat.

Please, let this work. It has to work. All around me there's the sound of engines, voices, and I lift my head just far enough to see through the windshield. The cars between me and the store roll away along with the rest, including mine. I peek out through the passenger window to see Murphy driving away with everyone else. It takes less than a minute for the area to clear out, until all that's left is the two cars already parked at the store and the Honda in which I'm hiding.

It's all up to him now.

I watch, my heart pounding, until the door opens an inch, then another. He's watching. Waiting. "Come on," I whisper, all of my attention trained on that door. "Come out. Come to me."

A man's head emerges—instantly, I know it's not him. This is not my guy. He's too young, skinny, and he looks terrified as he scans the area, then looks over his shoulder. Only then do I realize there's a hand on his shoulder—and most likely, a gun to the back of his head. Nelson sent him out first in case there were snipers.

There aren't any, and Nelson shoves the kid aside before emerging. This is my guy. I would know him anywhere, even though this is the first time I'm seeing his face. Tall, bulky, yet surprisingly fast on his feet for a man his size. He quicksteps his way across the pavement, his head swinging back-and-forth, the gun ready at his side. His curly, dark hair is soaked with sweat and the T-shirt he wears beneath an open coat has a dark patch on the chest.

I duck behind the front seat, my own gun at the ready. *Don't let him see me. Don't let him see me.* Either he doesn't look or I am hidden well enough that he doesn't notice. He's most likely too glad to open his car door unimpeded to notice anything out of the ordinary in his vehicle. He throws himself inside, his substantial weight making the car bounce, then drops his gun on the passenger seat before closing the door.

As soon as he does, I'm up, my gun pressed to his temple. "Don't move. Hands on the wheel. If you so much as lift a finger, it's over."

Red and blue lights color the night as the cars rush back onto the scene. The man in front of me is frozen stiff, his dark eyes wide in the rearview mirror. It isn't fear in those eyes. It's rage. I've seen both enough times to know the difference.

I shouldn't. But I have to. "It's nice to see you again," I whisper, my gaze trained on his reflection so I can register his understanding. "This time, there's no blizzard to help you escape." His face twitches and our eyes meet in the mirror. He knows. He understands.

"Hands! Let's see the hands!" One of the officers opens the door, weapon trained, and when Charles Nelson doesn't move fast enough, they drag him from the car. He crumbles onto the ground, gasping for air, groaning and weeping and cursing while he's handcuffed.

When I exit the car, it's not him I'm concerned with. It's the kid crouched against the convenience store wall, his hands fingers laced behind his neck while he shakes and sobs. One of the officers leads Jenny out, wrapped in his coat, leaning against him while she weeps brokenly.

It's over. They're alive and it's over.

And Charles Nelson knows I never stopped hunting him. He knows he didn't win.

34

"There you are!"

I barely have time to register the sound of Krista Duncan's voice before she's practically swallowed me in a fierce hug that leaves me wondering if my ribs will make it out intact. "Thank you, thank you. Thank you so much." Rob stands behind her, rubbing her shoulder, fighting back tears when our eyes meet.

"It's the least I could do," I whisper when emotion clogs my throat as well. "I wasn't about to let him go."

She leans back, her face red and slick with tears. "You really risked yourself. They told us on the way here, the officers who picked us up at home and drove us out here. They told us you got in that monster's car and waited for him. That was dangerous!"

"Don't forget she almost froze in a blizzard," Rob reminds her. "We shouldn't be surprised."

"I'm only sorry …" No. I shouldn't say it out loud. It's one thing for me to question my actions internally and another to vocalize them. They've got enough to think about and regret.

She won't let it go, though. "What? We understand it was too late by the time you found Cayden. There was nothing you could've done."

"That's not what I was thinking this time." I was thinking about how simple it would've been to put that evil man out of his misery with a single bullet. It was only me and him in that car. There would've been no one to contradict me if I claimed I felt threatened.

Rob gets it before she does. "No, you did the right thing," he murmurs, while gathering his wife into his arms. "If you had taken him out, we would never get to look him in the eye in the courtroom. That's what we want now. He doesn't deserve a quick and easy ending. He deserves to suffer, and that's exactly what he's going to do."

"Oh, yes," Krista agrees in a voice much firmer and stronger than before. "I can't wait to watch his sentencing. You made that possible. Thank you. Thank you for everything."

"You're welcome." Captain Felch emerges from his office and greets them, then guides them into his office to brief them on what happens next. We exchange a glance before he tips his head toward the front of the station. I know exactly what he's trying to say. Get out of here. You've done enough.

And for once, I am inclined to agree. I'm only half a dozen steps away before I pull up my phone and call Mitch. "Is that soup still hot?"

"IF ANYTHING, it benefited from sitting for an extra couple of hours." Mitch sops up was left in his bowl using a hunk of bread. "Not bad if I do say so myself."

"Not bad? It's incredible." Rich, flavorful, with a hint of pancetta adding a smoky note. "Maybe you should start selling soups at the café, too."

"Why don't I just open a restaurant?" he suggests, throwing his hands in the air. "Forget books."

I reach across his kitchen table and swat at him with my napkin. "No, don't forget books. And you can't run a restaurant on soup and baked goods alone." Though I tip my head to the side, thinking about it.

"Actually, I guess you could. But don't. The town needs a beautiful bookstore like yours."

His smile fades until it's more like a sad smirk. "What a shame you won't be here much longer to enjoy it."

I freeze with a piece of bread halfway between the bowl and my mouth. "Excuse me? Do you know something I don't know?"

"It was more of an assumption." When all I do is stare, waiting for more, he sighs like he's been put on the spot. "Well, you caught Cayden's murderer. Your sister's investigation is being worked out of the Portland field office. I imagined you would go out there, so you can be in the middle of everything. it just makes sense."

Maybe on paper. Yet when I consider leaving, nothing about the idea feels right. "Is that what you think I should do?" I venture, watching closely in the light from a candle flickering on the table. My stomach is fluttering and my palms feel sweaty, and I might as well be fifteen again. That's the age where it feels like your entire life hinges on what your crush will say.

Mitch frowns, setting the rest of his bread aside along with his empty bowl so he can fold his arms on the table. "Is it what you have to do? Let's start there."

"I'm not sure," I admit. "And that's the truth. I'm here because the Boston office sent me out here. The case was wrapped when I found Camille. The information in the cabin turned it into a different case—but not necessarily the case I was sent here for, if you get what I mean. I think it's going to depend on what my superiors decide."

"Sure. I know you don't necessarily have a say in these things." His gaze drifts down to the flickering candle, and I wish he would look at me, instead.

Might as well get it over with. "Do you want me to stay?" I blurt out before I can lose my nerve. To think, I hid in the back of a murderer's car earlier. I knew he was armed but I did it anyway. Hours later, I'm afraid to come out and ask a simple question while sitting in a cozy kitchen.

Mitch meets my gaze. "Yes." And that's it. There's no moment of hesitation, no need for him to think it over. The answer is right there. "Yes, I want you to stay. But I know you want to work the case, as well."

"Maybe I can do both. I want to."

"Yeah?" A smile begins to stir and hope dances in his eyes like the reflected candlelight. "You do?"

"Of course, I do. I want to be here. With you," I add in case he's not sure what I mean.

Then I look at my bowl. "I mean, first, I find out you can bake bread, then I find out you make a soup I would happily drink through a straw. Why would I pass up something like that?"

I dissolve into giggles when he groans and rolls his eyes. "And there I was, thinking about asking you to make our relationship official."

Like magic, my laughter dies. "Seriously?"

He cringes, shaking his head. "You don't have to ask like I suggested getting matching tattoos. Yes, seriously."

An official relationship. It's funny, but in my heart, we've been official all this time. I don't need a label. I know how I feel about him, and it's not going to change.

But I don't hate the idea of making it official, either. "Are you asking me to go steady?" I tease. "Are you going to write *Mitch + Alexis* on my locker? Maybe draw a heart around it?"

"You're starting to make me rethink this ..." When I swat at him again, he grabs my wrist and pulls me out of my chair until we're both leaning over the table. Let's be honest. I don't exactly make it difficult for him. "Yes. I want to go steady. I want to call you my girlfriend again."

We meet in the middle, beside the table, and I wind my arms around his waist. He runs a hand through my hair before gently cradling the back of my head. "What do you think about that?"

I pretend to think about it, but only for a few seconds. "I think I like the sound of it. Plus, you'd be doing me a favor."

His brows lift. "What do you mean?"

"As it turns out, I've been looking for a boyfriend, anyway."

35

It's a brilliant, beautiful morning, or maybe that's the brilliant, beautiful mood I'm in coloring the way I see things. Last night was hardly easy—at least, before Charles Nelson was captured. But everything after that was perfect, and I'm practically floating on air by the time I leave Mitch's house. My boyfriend's house. It's been more than ten years since I last called him that and I can't pretend it doesn't feel good. Like sliding into my favorite pair of jeans, the pair I know is going to fit like it was made for me every single time.

He let me sleep in, and I needed it. I didn't so much as crack an eyelid until it was well past nine o'clock, which for me may as well be a long, lazy sleep-in. He left breakfast to keep warm in the oven, a delicious plate of French toast and sausage patties. I'm feeling renewed by the time I get behind the wheel and call into the station.

Captain Felch answers on the first ring. "Tell me you're taking a breather today."

"Good morning to you, too. I'm not exactly going full force today, if that's what you mean."

"But you aren't staying home, either? Is this what I'm hearing? You hid out in an armed man's car last night. By the way, I'm not entirely sure what you were thinking, taking a risk like that. From the way I've heard it, the man was out of his mind."

"By then, he thought he'd gotten away with it." For someone so clever, he certainly fell for my scheme quickly enough. I guess it's one thing to kidnap and overpower a child and another to match wits with an adult—not to mention a dozen armed officers.

"You still risked yourself. Again."

"All in a day's work." The fact is, knowing Nelson is behind bars at this very minute has refocused me. If he can be brought to justice, so can the man we only know as Andrew Flynn.

Thinking of him brings me to my next subject, and the reason for my call. "Actually, I was thinking of visiting the family of the first kid who was killed. Blitzer, the name was. Her parents only live twenty minutes outside of town."

"You know," the captain reminds me, "you don't need to report to me anymore. The Bureau has taken over this case."

He's right. The strangest sense of something close to sadness steals a little of the color from this brilliant day. I've enjoyed working with him. But my job isn't with the Broken Hill police department.

To fill the sudden, awkward silence, I ask, "How about the Duncans? How were they by the time they left last night?"

"Heartbroken but pleased. They plan to attend the arraignment at ten o'clock. They got a room for the night in town."

"I'm glad for them. Did he confess?"

"It took three hours, but he finally broke down and admitted to Cayden's murder. He burned all the clothes he wore that night out in the woods, well behind the house. He took pains to be sure there was no evidence in the house for police to find." That would explain the lack of anything tying him to Cayden when we searched, after he made a run for it.

"There's one thing I don't quite understand." I turn the car onto Main Street and smile as I pass Mitch's shop. When I slow down, I can see him in there, standing behind the register and chatting with a customer. "Why was he all the way out here when the weather was supposed to be so bad?"

"According to him, he was one of Julian's regular customers. And he frequently purchased footage taken at those cabins in particular. He had been watching the family since they arrived the day before, and decided to get a room in town to be closer to them. He drove out to Lake Morgan the morning of, hoping to get a look at them in person. When he happened to find Cayden sledding alone …"

He couldn't resist the opportunity. I don't need to hear anymore. My curiosity has been satisfied. "So long as they have closure. I'm very relieved for them."

"Well … I suppose we'll play it by ear from here, wait and see what your next assignment will be."

"I've requested to be part of the investigation into what we found at the cabin. I'm not going anywhere if I can help it."

"I hope that's the case." With that, he ends the call and I reflect on how nice it is to be appreciated. It's not so much that I need praise, but rather that I sense his respect. It means the world, since I respect him, too.

I didn't expect to find both of the Blitzers at home at ten-thirty on a weekday, but there are two cars parked in the driveway when I come to a stop in front of a charming little ranch house nestled in the heart of a cluster of towering pines. There was a dusting of snow overnight, and the scene could be straight off the cover of an album of holiday music. What a shame I'm not here to talk about anything nearly that cheerful.

There's a man who looks to be in his mid-sixties sprinkling rock salt behind the parked cars, and he stops to shield his eyes from the sun when I open my door and step out. "Can I help you?" he calls out to me.

"Hi, there." I raise a hand in greeting, moving slowly toward him in hopes he doesn't get spooked. "Are you Mr. Blitzer?"

"Mark Blitzer, that's me." He lost his daughter nearly three decades ago, when he was in his mid-thirties. Now he looks to be at retirement age yet clearly stays in shape. "And who might you be?"

The front door to the house opens and out steps a woman whose shoulder-length silver curls seem to sparkle in the sunlight. "Mark?" she calls out, wrapping her arms around herself to ward off the chill.

"It's okay, Susan," he calls back, still staring at me.

I'm guessing they don't get a lot of surprise visitors. "I'm sorry, I should've introduced myself. My name is Alexis Forrest. I'm an FBI agent, but I've been working on cases in Broken Hill as of late. I'm here to talk to you about Crystal, if you don't mind."

"Crystal?" Mark's head snaps back before it snaps around so he can find his wife, still standing on the porch. Her eyes go wide and she rocks back on her heels, staring at me.

"I am so sorry if it's a shock," I offer.

Mrs. Blitzer shakes off her surprise. "If it's a shock, it's because we never expected anybody to ever come to us about her. We've sort of been on our own."

"Why don't you come inside?" Mark offers. There's no longer that wary, suspicious note in his voice. "Maybe you'd like something hot to drink? It's a cold one out here."

"Thank you. I would appreciate something hot." I follow him up the drive, carefully scraping my boots along the welcome mat to dislodge any salt from the soles before stepping into a house that can only be described as cozy. A fire crackles away and warms the air, while the aroma of apples and cinnamon waft in from the kitchen. "I have a cake in the oven," Susan explains. "There's fresh coffee in the pot. Right this way."

We go to the kitchen, and Mark hangs his coat on a hook by the back door before sitting with me at the table. There are checkered curtains on the window matching the checkered tablecloth. It's a sweet little home. I can only imagine it's felt rather empty without Crystal.

"You said you were sort of on your own when it comes to Crystal? What does that mean?"

Susan exchanges a glance with her husband before bringing the coffee to the table, along with a little pitcher of creamer and a bowl of sugar. "We haven't heard from the local police in years," she explains with a soft, weary sigh before lowering herself into one of the chairs. Like her husband, she seems healthy, fit. But there's sadness bracketing the corners of her mouth, and Mark reaches for her hand on top of the table.

"We still call every year, on the anniversary of her disappearance," Mark explains in a gruff voice. Unlike his wife, he's kept much of the rich, dark brown color in his hair, but the same sadness is etched in every line of his face. "Of course, they never have anything new for us."

"It was such a nightmare," Susan murmurs, fixing herself a cup and stirring it loudly before tapping the spoon on the rim of the mug. "Everything is a blur. How can a person disappear like that without a trace, without a clue left behind until the body is found?"

"It felt very much like the police were overwhelmed, and under-concerned," Mark tells me flat-out. "I'm sorry, but it's true. I'm not trying to insult anyone."

"Believe me, I understand," I tell him. "I grew up in Broken Hill, which is just as quiet as your area. I know the local police there aren't generally prepared for a crime like this. It just doesn't happen."

"But it did happen," Susan reminds me. "And it felt very much like no one around here seemed particularly interested in finding answers."

"If you're from Broken Hill, what brings you out here?" Mark asks.

"I'm investigating a case that looks more and more like it involves the work of a serial killer." I speak slowly, carefully, choosing my words based upon their reactions. They both take a quick breath at the mention of a serial killer but manage to keep quiet. "And I believe Crystal was one of his victims."

Susan takes a shuddering breath while her husband asks, "What makes you think that?"

"I was investigating the disappearance of Camille Martin." I give them a brief, rundown – they both seem familiar with the case, which I guess they would be. It was all over the news. "The cabin in which Camille was held contained information on other disappearances. Other murders. Crystal was one of the victims whose articles and photos were displayed on the walls."

"Oh, my goodness." Susan sets down her mug and reaches again for her husband's hand.

Mark takes a deep breath. "Was there anything else about her there? Something belonging to her, that kind of thing?"

"There was a lot of evidence at the cabin," I tell him, "but I don't know about anything specific like that. Though it does seem after thirty years ..." I don't have the heart to finish my thought.

It doesn't seem like I need to. His shoulders fall along with his face. "Of course. I was hoping, that's all."

"I understand. And I know ..." No, I can't tell him about Maddie. Not now, probably not ever. They don't need to know about that connection. "I know you want closure. I would like to see that you get it. I want to reopen her case, along with the other cases documented in the cabin."

"And the cabin was in Broken Hill, you said?" Mark asks.

"Yes, right around the edge of town, deep in the woods. At one time, it was part of a cluster of cabins used by hunters during the season."

They exchange a look I don't understand before Mark asks, "Is it near Builders Creek?"

"Yes, now that you mention it. Builders Creek marks the western edge of the property." And if Camille had found it, she could have followed it straight to the road and been there in less than an hour. Unfortunately, she went in the opposite direction. "Why do you ask?"

"Oh … Oh, no …" Susan covers her mouth with one hand and the color drains from her face. I watch, dumbfounded, as her eyes fill with tears.

Mark clears his throat. His complexion has also gone an alarming shade of white. "I might still have pictures somewhere."

He gets up from the table while I wait, confused, wishing I could comfort his wife. She hasn't said a word or even made a sound except for a few stifled whimpers. Mark returns a moment later, holding a handful of envelopes full of pictures that he lays out on the table before sifting through them. "I know I have them somewhere. It was that last trip we took …"

Then he pulls a photo from a stack and slaps it onto the table in front of me. "Is that it? Is that the place?"

Thirty years have passed, but some things don't change. Like the creek running alongside the cabin only a few dozen yards away. It's cleaner, in much better condition, but I recognize it right off. "I think so. If not that exact cabin, it's on the property."

Susan stands and Mark wraps her in a hug. "That was where we took our last vacation together," she explains in a shaky, tearful voice. "Only a few months before Crystal died."

EPILOGUE

Epilogue - Someone's watching

THERE SHE IS.

My pulse races as I sit and watch a young woman leave my cabin. Her shoulders are pulled up around her ears and she's breathing hard, heavy, one cloud after another rising up from her pretty, pink lips. I noticed those lips right away, the first time I saw her. It's sort of a habit, noticing little things like that. Features, body parts. Sometimes, things jump out at me.

I didn't know who she was that first time, when she stopped me on campus. She was just another pretty young thing out of so many others I ran into every day. It was like being in front of a buffet, working at that school. So many options to choose from. I saw her name in the logbook at the guard house later that day—some people might have balked right away, might have run once an FBI agent showed up in their hunting grounds, sniffing around, asking questions. That wasn't what interested me.

It was her name. Alexis Forrest. We have somebody in common, she and I. An old friend who connects us.

Weeks later, my satisfaction hasn't ebbed. It washes over me now and makes me smile while I watch from a distance using my binoculars. She's determined, this one. She thinks she's going to find me. So many people have labored under the same delusion, but none have been successful, have they? The years have passed and the faces have changed, but I have remained. I'm the only constant.

She shoves her hands into her pockets and tips her head back to stare up at the sky. What is she thinking of? Her sister? Is she asking for guidance from that sweet angel? Every time I notice the thin scars on my right forearm, I remember that angel scratching me in those final moments when she gave it her all. I even admired that, though it was sort of inconvenient at the time. But I'm glad for it now. I've been glad ever since. In a sense, Maddie is always with me.

"You think you know me, don't you?" I wait until she's moving to start my engine and follow her progress toward the road. She'll head back to town now—she's nothing if not predictable. But I appreciate that. It makes my work easier, being able to predict what someone's going to do. And unless my instincts are suddenly off, she'll go to her boyfriend's house now. Occasionally, she goes to the house where she grew up, but she's been spending more time with him lately.

When her Corolla passes, pointed toward town, I know I'm right. I wait a few beats, then turn onto Route 1 and follow her at a safe distance. I had to ditch the truck, figuring she'd be looking for it, so she doesn't give a second thought to my dark gray SUV if she even notices me in her mirror. I doubt she would. She's looking forward to seeing her boyfriend.

But I am on her mind, too. Me and her beautiful sister. We spent a lot of time together, me and Maddie. I know things about her that Alexis could never guess. We became quite intimate, in fact. She interested me. They very rarely do once I've got them with me, but she was different. She was special.

Just like her little sister.

So she knows about me. She knows about the business I've conducted in my cabin all these years.

But there are things she doesn't know, things no one knows. Only me. I've considered cluing her in, giving her an idea of exactly who she's dealing with and how long I've been at this. And how many other cabins there have been. How many more final breaths I've witnessed. It would shock her to her core.

The idea excites me, but I can't give in. Not yet. Not when it's so much fun watching her. Getting to know her. I even admire her in my own way. She's smart. Not smart enough to realize who she was talking to when she asked me for directions, but nobody's perfect.

"You think you can find me?" I whisper as she comes to a stop at a house that's now become familiar to me after following her here so many times. Sitting outside, gazing up at the windows, imagining what's happening behind them. That fellow of hers doesn't seem like much, but then there's no accounting for taste. My own taste hasn't always served me well, but that's the thing about women. Things might not work out with one, but there's always another on the way. Like waiting for a train. Women have come and gone over the decades. Wives, girlfriends. I even have at least one kid out there that I know of, though we are strangers and always have been.

But my work? My work has been my only constant. The hunt. The thrill of it. Coming so close, never being detected. Existing on the fringes, overlooked, disregarded—until I decide to show myself. Until I decide to strike.

"Don't worry, little Alexis," I whisper as she climbs from her car and heads up to the house, where the front door opens before she's reached it so her lovesick puppy of a boyfriend can greet her with a hug. "I won't show myself yet. Have a nice night with your boyfriend, and sleep well."

Because the fun is going to start soon.

THANK for you reading Forest of Shadow. Can't wait to find out what happens to Alexis next? **Grab Forest of Secrets now!**

Forest of Shadows

Forensic psychologist and FBI agent Alexis Forrest's search for the serial killer responsible for her sister's murder has hit a wall. All the evidence she has found has led her to the identities of numerous victims, yet the killer is still unknown.

But he knows who she is, and he is watching her from the shadows. He is hiding in plain sight near Broken Hill, the snowy New England town that Alexis used to call home.

Meanwhile, a young suburban mother goes missing while out on a morning run. When Alexis starts to dig deeper, she finds out that the woman's perfect marriage and family are not what they seem. Secrets and resentments are swirling around the couple. Did someone take her or was it the husband after all?

While Alexis is busy with her new case, the serial killer continues to watch. He is close. Close enough to strike.

Can Alexis find the woman before she's killed? Can she figure out who is stalking her before he makes his move?

1-CLICK FOREST OF SECRETS NOW!

IF YOU ENJOYED THIS BOOK, please don't forget to leave a review on Amazon and Goodreads! Reviews help me find new readers.

If you have any issues with anything in the book or find any typos, please email me at Kate@kategable.com. Thank you so much for reading!

ALSO CHECK out my other bestselling and 3 time Silver Falchion award winning series, **Girl Missing.**

When her 13-year-old sister vanishes on her way back from a friend's house, Detective Kaitlyn Carr must confront demons from her own past in order to bring her sister home.

The small mountain town of Big Bear Lake is only three hours away but a world

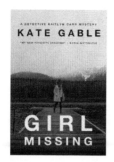

away from her life in Los Angeles. It's the place she grew up and the place that's plagued her with lies, death and secrets.

As Kaitlyn digs deeper into the murder that she is investigating and her sister's disappearance, she finds out that appearances are misleading and few things are what they seem.

A murderer is lurking in the shadows and the more of the mystery that Kaitlyn unspools the closer she gets to danger herself.

Can Kaitlyn find the killer and solve the mystery of her sister's disappearance before it's too late?

What happens when someone else is taken?

1-click Girl Missing now!

ABOUT KATE GABLE

Kate Gable loves a good mystery that is full of suspense. She grew up devouring psychological thrillers and crime novels as well as movies, tv shows and true crime.

Her favorite stories are the ones that are centered on families with lots of secrets and lies as well as many twists and turns. Her novels have elements of psychological suspense, thriller, mystery and romance.

Kate Gable lives near Palm Springs, CA with her husband, son, a dog and a cat. She has spent more than twenty years in Southern California and finds inspiration from its cities, canyons, deserts, and small mountain towns.

She graduated from University of Southern California with a Bachelor's degree in Mathematics. After pursuing graduate studies in mathematics, she switched gears and got her MA in Creative Writing and English from Western New Mexico University and her PhD in Education from Old Dominion University.

Writing has always been her passion and obsession. Kate is also a USA Today Bestselling author of romantic suspense under another pen name.

Write her here:

Kate@kategable.com

Check out her books here:

www.kategable.com

Sign up for my newsletter:
https://www.subscribepage.com/kategableviplist

Join my Facebook Group:
https://www.facebook.com/groups/
833851020557518

Bonus Points: Follow me on BookBub and Goodreads!

https://www.bookbub.com/authors/kate-gable

https://www.goodreads.com/author/show/21534224.Kate_Gable

- amazon.com/Kate-Gable/e/B095XFCLL7
- facebook.com/KateGableAuthor
- bookbub.com/authors/kate-gable
- instagram.com/kategablebooks
- tiktok.com/@kategablebooks

ALSO BY KATE GABLE

Detective Kaitlyn Carr Psychological Mystery series
Girl Missing (Book 1)
Girl Lost (Book 2)
Girl Found (Book 3)
Girl Taken (Book 4)
Girl Forgotten (Book 5)
Gone Too Soon (Book 6)
Gone Forever (Book 7)
Whispers in the Sand (Book 8)

Girl Hidden (FREE Novella)

Detective Charlotte Pierce Psychological Mystery series
Last Breath
Nameless Girl

Missing Lives
Girl in the Lake

Made in the USA
Monee, IL
01 March 2024